Cynthia d'Entremont

UNLOCKED

A Novel

To Daniela,
Enjoy life's journey!
Cynthia d'Entremont

UNLOCKED

Published by Word Alive Press

WORD ALIVE PRESS
Just Write!

131 Cordite Road, Winnipeg, Manitoba, R3W 1S1
www.wordalivepress.ca

Printed in Canada

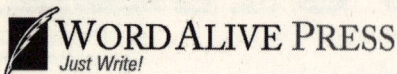

For Joshua and Elianna,
Keep the key with you always ...
And for those who are searching,
May you find home.

Contents

1
The Heaps

Jaron gobbled the scraps of pork fat, licking his fingers so he wouldn't miss a morsel. He knew his thirst would rage later—indulging in such a salty feast came at a high price. But he hadn't survived ten year-spans at the Garbage Heaps by being choosy.

A newly dumped Five-Year with a stained shirt and snotty nose waddled past him. "One for one," the child said, eyeing Jaron's pork scraps while tightly grasping his own half-eaten biscuit.

"You'll make it to Leaving Day for sure," Jaron said under his breath, glancing at the watchtower and finding the guard's eyes upon them.

"One for one. Each one stands alone. Only the strong survive." Jaron uttered the only words Heapdwellers were allowed to speak to one another. Even though he no longer felt hungry, he snatched his remaining scraps of food. Maybe he'd have a chance to slip them to Devora later on when the guards weren't looking.

Trudging toward the lower border of the Heaps, Jaron searched for any liquid that was fit to drink. Often, when he foraged down here, he would take the chance to sneak glances at the White Palace towering high above the cinderblock wall.

1

"Dirty rat," Jaron swore when he noticed Benjamin only a few arm-spans away busily gnawing at a mouldy husk of corn.

Benjamin ignored him until a gull bouncing off one of the White Palace's sparkling windows attracted his scowling attention. "You know who lives there, don't you?" Benjamin muttered, his lips barely moving.

"No more than you do," Jaron replied, sifting absent-mindedly through the rubble in an attempt to mask their conversation from the guards. His eyes tracked the spiralling descent of the wounded bird until it plummeted out of sight behind the cinderblock barrier. He cringed at the spectacle of the gull's crimson blood trickling down onto the spotless windowsill.

"I know because I heard them—the guards. They didn't see me burrowing over by the drawbridge this morning."

"Liar," Jaron said, his heart pounding. Anyone discovered eavesdropping on the guards got hauled away, never to return.

"Am not!" Benjamin said, his voice growing louder. "I heard the guards say it's where they keep *them*!"

"Them, who?"

"Them, the Chosen—with their Holding Shells."

"I don't believe you," Jaron said quietly, picking his way through the trash with his back to the watchtower to shield his moving lips. Benjamin was speaking too loudly, being careless. What was wrong with him? It was like he didn't care about surviving until Leaving Day.

"I can prove it," Benjamin said, unfolding a white slip of paper.

"Put that away!" Jaron whispered. If the guards saw them talking, sharing information …

Suddenly a guard crested the trash pile right behind Benjamin, and Jaron uttered a hurried, "One for one." In the Heaps, guilt by association earned the same punishment as being guilty.

"I knew I'd catch you breaking the rules sooner or later," the guard said, locking chains around Benjamin's wrists. "Think you can steal from us and get away with it?" He turned to Jaron and stared for a moment before saying, "Get out of here now, rodent. I've half a mind to take you too."

"I curse you, Jaron!" Benjamin cried out, struggling to break away from the guard's grasp. "You're a needy little Squealing Bundle!"

Jaron squatted with his back toward them and closed his eyes to shut out Benjamin's shrinking reflection haunting him from a shiny chunk of metal. His relief at not being caught shamed him. He reached for the key he kept hidden under his shirt and discovered that it was exposed. It must have slipped out when he was digging through the trash. Had the guard noticed? His hand closed over the key and he focused on a faraway memory—a wisp of a dream.

Lullaby and good night, the dream whispered, barely blooming into focus before it slipped away into the putrid waste around him.

He knew only stolen bits about what happened outside the boundaries of the cinderblock walls. Benjamin's news of the Holding Shells and the Chosen made his stomach swirl like he had eaten too many maggots. The Holding Shells were the ones who forgot the faces of their babies, the Squealing Bundles that eventually ended up at the Garbage Heaps.

Did they really dance about the White Palace eating first-day food until their bellies swelled out like plump rat mamas? Did they, too, give birth to a whole litter and then only keep the best one?

"You were not chosen," Jaron whispered. Every morning when the sun cast its first splash of warmth across the Heaps, the rusty loud speakers blasted this truth to the waking refuse—the Heapdwellers. Every one of them had been cast aside while the Holding Shells scampered about with the Chosen.

Some newly dumped Five-Years would screech, "No! No! I want Mama!" and stamp their mud-caked toes until they ended up as tiny sobbing mounds mixing drool with slime from the Heaps.

The other Heapdwellers ignored them, chanting, "One for one. Each one stands alone. Only the strong survive."

After a few days, the Five-Years mumbled the words right along with all of the others. Sweet-smelling mamas were dreams that faded, replaced by the cold truth about Holding Shells.

Later in the day, Jaron scavenged some bananas that still had a few yellow spots on them. His hunger slightly abated, he crept inside his shelter for the night. It wasn't long before he heard the patter of rain begin softly and then increase to a hammering torrent.

He tried not to think about the newly dumped Five-Years, wet and shivering without a shelter. *No guilt*, he chanted over and over in his head. *No guilt—one for one.*

"Jaron," a voice called out, barely audible over the rain drumming against the tin roof of his shelter.

Instinct made him reach for the shard of glass he'd fashioned into a weapon.

"Jaron!"

"I'm here, Devora," he whispered, startled that she would risk visiting him. Squeezing to one side of his hovel, he swept away the cockroaches that had scurried in to escape the downpour.

Her chilled damp skin pressed against his arm.

"You shouldn't be here. It isn't safe." Jaron knew she must stay only for a few moments—even in the rain, the guards patrolled the darkness, searching for violators.

She spoke barely above a whisper. "They took Benjamin today."

Jaron shrugged.

"Don't pretend it doesn't matter!" she said, her voice growing louder.

"Why should it? Benjamin hates me." He pulled himself away from her, no longer able to stand the gentle warmth now emanating from her thin body.

"You used to be different," Devora hissed. "Don't you remember? Benjamin came to the Heaps the same day you and I did."

Of course he remembered that day. The three of them had huddled together in the rain until a guard finally scattered them with the threat of a beating.

Despite the rules, they had secretly banded together over their ten year-spans in the Heaps. They watched out for one another, depositing little treats in a covert hiding spot in case the others hadn't scavenged enough food for the day, nodding and blinking signals in their own private code that the guards never detected. Regularly, on the night of the tiniest sliver of moon, they would gather together to share fragmented tales of an outside world.

Devora's voice grew hard. "Benjamin couldn't forgive you for the trick you played on him to steal his shelter."

"I had to do it, Devora, believe me," he said, wondering why she didn't hate Benjamin too.

She pulled herself away from him. "I don't believe anything you say anymore," she said before darting out into the rain.

Too late he remembered the horded bits of food he'd wanted to share with her. "One for one," he whispered, his voice drowned out by the rain.

"You were not chosen," the Heapdwellers chanted in unison the following morning. Jaron regurgitated the mantra along with the others as the words flashed across the viewing screen and an amplified voice boomed the repetitive morning message. "One for one. Each one stands alone. Only the strong survive."

The letters of the alphabet popped up on the screen and Jaron mumbled the lesson along with the others. "'B' is for ball, 'C' is for cat ..."

Then there were letters strung together to make a longer sound—a word. Today's words all contained the "O" sound. The lessons became progressively more difficult throughout the morning, and soon the younger Heapdwellers began to stare blankly at the screen, forcing themselves to pay attention.

Sit still, Jaron mentally instructed when he noticed a Five-Year girl beginning to fidget.

A guard marched over to her and struck her arm with his whip. She winced and gripped where she'd been hit but held back her outcry of pain.

Good girl, Jaron thought, watching out of the corner of his eye as silent tears slid down her cheeks. If she had yelped, the guard would have thrashed her again.

Jaron had stopped puzzling about why he needed to learn how to read after he scavenged his first book year-spans ago. The stories would carry him to a faraway land, igniting his imagination and making him dream of open spaces free from garbage and rats. But then he'd wake up and find himself still there, in the Heaps.

He also occasionally discovered fragments of newspapers that told strange tales of another place—a place beyond the cinderblock walls. And there were pictures of people sitting and eating together, smiling and holding hands, accompanied by stories of "parties" at a place called Lord Drake's castle.

The stories must be pretend—like the Fairyland Devora believed in. Nothing like that ever happened here.

Staring up at the only structure visible over the walls of the Heaps, Jaron wondered if Benjamin might have been right about the White Palace being where the Holding Shells lived.

"Pay attention!" A guard ordered, snapping a short whip across Jaron's arm.

Pain.

Often it was the only thing that made Jaron feel alive, although it did nothing to help him decide if he was awake. Dreams and nightmares often collided within his reality. Somehow, though, at this moment he guessed he'd only been daydreaming.

The lesson ended with a list. Leaving Day names. His and Devora's names flashed across the screen. It had come without warning. Tomorrow evening before the breaking of the New Moon, he and Devora would leave the Heaps—and go where?

His damp clothing clung to his skin as he walked back to his shelter, counting the number of scavengers within view. Sixty-two. And that was on just one mountain of trash. The Heaps consisted of dozens of mountains and hundreds of "not chosen."

"And probably millions of cockroaches," he muttered as one scuttled over his big toe and another crawled up his leg. He burrowed into his shelter to escape the blaze of the noonday sun. Glancing around his makeshift home, he realized that tomorrow he would be saying good-bye to the only thing he could call his own.

Unfolding a torn strip of newspaper, he whispered, "Home for sale." He traced his finger along the words printed in black. The picture displayed a gleaming white shelter with shiny windows, a speckled roof, and a red door.

Maybe after Leaving Day he'd find a door like that—one with a lock his key would open. Not like the solitary black door embedded in the boundary wall of the Heaps. Once, year-spans ago, he'd worked up the courage to tug on the handle of that door. Of course it had been locked. He'd tried his key, but to no avail.

He slowed his breathing and listened as the rustling of footsteps approached his shelter.

Crunch. Rattle. Crunch. Then nothing.

"Give me a light, would ya?"

Jaron knew the deep voice belonged to one of the guards—the hairy-faced one.

He heard the scrape of the match and imagined the two guards puffing on cigars as they talked unaware of Jaron nearby, camouflaged by his shelter.

"It's a sorry bunch of program failures leaving tomorrow," the hairy-faced guard said.

"What a waste. This group only had one pass. What was his name again?"

"I don't know. Ben—something."

"Right. Benjamin. He got out of here just in time. Yesterday. Right down to the wire. Only two days before his Leaving Day."

Jaron gulped the sour air. Benjamin? Benjamin had passed? Dizzy, he closed his eyes.

"Too bad the other garbage rats are too stupid to figure out how things work around here," the hairy-faced guard added.

The other guard replied, "Yeah. You'd think Lord Drake would find another way to train his Enforcers."

The sound of the guards' fading footsteps let Jaron know that they had moved away from his shelter. He and Devora had almost made it to Leaving Day, not Benjamin! For ten year-spans he had followed the rules. Well, most of them, anyway. The biggest rule had been the one nobody had spoken aloud—don't get caught breaking the rules.

Jaron squeezed his eyes tighter to stop the spinning as he stumbled from his shelter. He had to do something.

"Have you seen Devora?" he growled at a Five-Year who was sucking on a hardened chunk of mouldy bread.

The boy's eyes widened before he cowered to the ground, a shivering lump amongst pickle jars, bread bags, and carrot peels. Jaron groaned at the sight of the fresh jagged wounds sliced across the child's back.

"Devora! DEVORA!" Jaron shouted, his heart racing. The rusty giant claw roared to life and started scooping trash from outside the cinderblock walls and scattering it over the living, breathing mountains of the Heaps. At first he sighed, thankful that no guards would hear him yell amidst the scraping metal. But then he feared Devora wouldn't hear him over the noise either. Stomping over the next pile of trash, he thought his insides would burst. He needed to find her before it was too late.

"DEVORA!" He was screaming now, not absorbing the sudden quiet. The metal claw that had been chugging and slurping suddenly slouched in silence. Startled scavengers bobbed up out of the trash and stared at him, forcing him to gulp back his next outcry.

A movement from behind the shadow of a broken, rusted vehicle caught his eye. "Devora," he mouthed, relieved she was so near.

She put her finger to her lips. *Shush*, she was gesturing. *Shush*, her eyes were pleading.

What the guards said can't be true. Jaron wavered, watching Devora and the others meekly obeying the rules. He'd been sequestered here for ten year-spans, waiting for his promised Leaving Day. Wouldn't he have heard some whispered rumour before today? Some hint at the uselessness of it all?

"Leaving Day is for failures," he ventured, forcing his lips to stay motionless as he spoke. "I overheard the guards. They said Benjamin passed and we're the failures!"

Devora kept silent. A guard's whip cracked in the distance.

"Not here," she finally responded, bending over to sort through the freshly dumped food scraps already buzzing with flies. "Tonight, at the culvert. It's the night of the smallest moon."

"Tonight," he agreed, his thoughts drifting to Benjamin again. The three of them used to gather at the culvert under the blackest of skies ... until that unspeakable night only four new moons ago. None of them had met there since. He shuddered and hoped he could convince her that everything they believed was a lie.

But first he had to convince himself.

2

The Darkest Night

Leafing through the damp pile of newspaper clippings, Jaron searched for the photographs. "Here's one," he whispered to himself, scanning a caption: *Lord Drake invites Duke Ubel of Corwyn City to Enforcers Graduation.*

Enforcers.

Only a short time ago the guards had spoken of Lord Drake's Enforcers. An icy fist gripped Jaron's heart. *Was it true, then? Were all these stories true?* He scattered the papers across the muddy floor of his shelter. The captions leapt off the pages, mocking his ten year-spans of compliance. *Enforcers Increase Productivity at Plakin Mine. Enforcers Bring Safety to the Streets of Corwyn City. Enforcers Crush Underground Movement.*

Did the Enforcers bring safety to the world outside the Heaps?

The New Moons had crept by slowly, stretching time into tortured year-spans. And never, in those endless days, had mercy been shown to the residents of the Heaps. How could the abandonment and isolation of this place serve as training for such a noble duty?

Jaron reminisced about a stolen moment when he'd once quietly wiped away the tears of a Five-Year. Could that be what Enforcers were meant to learn? Kindness?

Pressing his hand to his temple, he recalled Benjamin's venomous words. How did rabid hatred qualify Benjamin to be an Enforcer?

Despite year-spans of practice arguing with himself, Jaron's stomach quivered as he mentally rehearsed how he'd present his evidence to Devora. Would she believe him?

He folded the newspaper clippings together and tucked them inside a small sack he'd scavenged long ago. Like everything else fashioned of cloth that landed in the Heaps, the sack had eventually turned from its vibrant colour to a dim shade of murky brown. He added a small pack of precious matches and a candle stub to serve as a light inside the culvert. If Devora could see proof in black and white, she'd understand.

The sun faded and Jaron set out toward the lower border of the Heaps. He travelled the majority of the distance aided by the pale glow of the sunset spilling over the ugliness that surrounded him. Just before reaching the runoff sludge, he picked a spot to burrow into some trash to wait for the sky to blacken. Moving throughout the Heaps in darkness was not permitted—a rule often broken without pain of penalty if one was careful.

And he *must* be careful. He'd be breaking three rules tonight: traveling after dark, going across the sludge into the culvert, and speaking with Devora.

But if failure is really passing, maybe I should let myself get caught …

In the twilight Jaron allowed himself a brief, wry grin.

Dim stars dotted the night sky. On the night of the New Moon, and for many days after, the pale stars could not compete at all with their brighter cousin. But tonight, on the Darkest Night, the stars shone modestly clear. It was as if they understood that this was their moment of glory.

The water in the culvert was knee-deep; the rains from the night before still filtering through the waste of the Heaps and making their enviable path of escape through the concrete tunnel. Iron bars midway through the passage prevented the Heapdwellers from enjoying that same freedom. And to make doubly sure that waif-like Five-Years wouldn't find a way to squeeze through the narrow openings, guards patrolled the area during the day.

But they didn't bother to check the culvert at night. Maybe they thought the Heapdwellers couldn't stomach the furry blanket of rats that teemed through the waters. Or maybe it was the guards that couldn't tolerate the rats. Either way, Jaron, Devora, and Benjamin had discovered year-spans ago that they could seek a brief refuge here.

At the iron bars, Jaron struck a match and the candlewick sprung to life. Instantly, the rats scattered.

"I'm relieved you were here first," Devora said as she arrived a few minutes later. "I hate it when the water is this high."

Watching her rub her bare arms for warmth, he wondered what she would look like if she were unsoiled and dressed lavishly like the women at Lord Drake's parties. He held the stack of photographs near the candle's flame. "I think these prove what I heard today is true."

"How can it be?" She sifted through the photos, tracing the images with her torn, blackened fingernail.

Shaking his head, he said, "I don't know. I always thought these stories were pretend. Maybe from another world. But now—"

"There are no girls in this picture," she said, pointing to the uniformed Enforcers at their graduation.

"I didn't notice … that."

"Of course not," she spat.

"But there must be something for girls too. In our group just Benjamin passed. Maybe the girls usually—"

"What?" She cut him off, sparks flaring in her eyes—a fire more intense than simply the reflection of the candle's flame.

He answered, "I don't know, but I think we should try and get caught. Tonight."

"No."

"I want to be one, Devora. An Enforcer. I want to help people be safe."

She clamped her lips together. "You never cared about that in the Heaps."

The accusation hung between them like a dank fog, cold and heavy. How could she say that? She knew the rules.

"Please come with me," he said.

"No," she repeated through clenched teeth. "Tomorrow is my Leaving Day. I won't throw it all away. Not after everything I've … survived."

He masked his regret at her choice. He would go where she would go, but right now he couldn't seem to speak the promise aloud. Instead, he snuffed out the candle. "We should find shelter for the night."

Quietly, they slipped back across the runoff sludge. "Take these," he said, handing her the sack filled with photos. "There's still time to decide before we leave at sundown—"

"Stop! I won't change my mind," she whispered, clutching at the sack.

"Until tomorrow, then," he replied, waiting silently as she slipped away to find a burrowing place for the night.

He stared at the stars, wondering what they were. New worlds? Distant candles? The morning message never talked about the stars, only the New Moon and how it shifted Leviathon's days into nights and propelled the sun to grow food.

As he ventured forward, his foot slid out from under him and he stumbled back, splashing into the sludge. He waited in the darkness, not daring even to breath. *Please think I'm a rat taking a midnight swim.*

A light as powerful as the searing noonday sun blinded him.

"You there!" a guard shouted. "Stand up!"

Jaron felt a hand clamp around the back of his neck. He lifted his arm to defend himself but instantly dropped it. Maybe the distant stars had powers after all. Maybe they'd heard his secret cry for escape.

"Devora, they've caught me! Come too. Please!" he called out, hearing his own panicked voice. Was she still nearby or had she made it all the way back to her shelter?

No answer.

The guard's grip tightened. "You weren't alone?" he growled, bobbing the light across the garbage.

She *was* there—close. Jaron saw her hand still gripping his sack and his heart leapt with hope. But she didn't flinch and the guard didn't seem to take notice of her.

Then he knew. She wasn't coming with him.

"You can keep my things!" he said, wishing it wasn't too late. Wishing he could stay with her, protect her. "Take my books! Especially the red one—it's your favourite."

"Shut up, you crazy rat," the guard shouted. "There's no one listening to you now."

Flashing the light ahead of them, the guard shoved Jaron over the piles of garbage and toward the single door that promised escape.

One more day, Jaron thought. One more day and he would have made it to Leaving Day, the unknown prize he had dreamed of while shivering night after night. The unknown prize that he now believed spelled failure.

Whatever the Garbage Heaps had trained him for, whatever being an Enforcer meant, he had made it—with no time to spare. His only regret was that Devora had been too scared to join him.

3

Lady of Light

Devora inched her head over the garbage and caught a final glimpse of light as Jaron and the guard vanished. For the last ten year-spans her world had been made up of two people: Benjamin and Jaron. Now both were gone.

Throughout the night, she shivered in and out of consciousness, sleep never really taking hold. By dawn her limbs were chilled and her head ached. She picked her way over the Heaps and stood before the black door marked "Authorized Personnel Only." She hadn't seen it happen, but she knew this was where Jaron had exited only hours ago. Staring at the ground, she wondered if his footprints might still be visible in the mud.

The door burst open and Devora felt like her insides had wings. They had made a mistake and were bringing Jaron back ...

Her heart landed with a thud. A guard entered, depositing three new Five-Years on a heap of trash a few arm-spans from the door. Two boys and a girl. A bitter resemblance to herself, Jaron, and Benjamin ten year-spans earlier.

One of the new Five-Years marched off, full of purpose. Stupid thing! It wouldn't take long for him to discover that life in the Heaps had no purpose. Even if the relentless morning message didn't hammer into his head a sense of worthlessness, scavenging in rotting garbage would soon get the point across. The second boy wandered off, leaving the girl alone.

"It's better that way," Devora whispered. If she'd been alone from the beginning she wouldn't be standing here feeling like her insides had been ripped out. Waiting. Waiting for a door to open. Waiting for an impossible wish to come true.

She crossed her arms and hugged herself. She didn't believe in wishes … or fairies. Not anymore. Not since that night …

Shuddering, she set her lips in a firm line. How could Jaron have left her here, unprotected? She knew he'd seen her swollen face the day he'd stolen Benjamin's shelter. His eyes had betrayed him. But he hadn't said one word—not then, not ever. Even as the cut above her lip had faded to a jagged scar and the gulf of silent anger divided her two friends, Jaron had said nothing.

"It's true, little girl. You are alone."

Devora whirled around. The sound of the whispered voice had chilled her, yet she longed to hear more. "Who are you?" she stammered, staring at the most extraordinary person she'd ever seen. A woman with golden lights bouncing off pale yellow hair and silken white skin stood before her.

The stranger wasn't a Heapdweller—they were covered with years of muck and garbage that clung like an extra skin infiltrated only by lice and rats nibbling persistently through the layers.

Squinting, Devora opened her mouth to speak but then quickly remembered the rules. "One for one," she said, turning away.

The glowing figure reached out and clasped Devora's arm. "They can't see me now. Only those who are truly alone can. I've come to help you."

Devora refused to listen to this trick her mind was playing on her. A person no one else could see? Talking to someone who wasn't there? She really must go back to her shelter and collect her things. Maybe have a morning nap. If she wasn't careful, she'd be the next one pulled through the black door against her will. She would *not* lose it all only hours away from the end.

"Trust me."

Trust? What was trust? Devora shut her eyes and tried to recall any morning lessons about trust. Nothing. She imagined it would be spelled t-r-u-s-t. "'T' is for tack," she muttered, picturing a sharp, pointed object with a flat head to push on.

"I am Solange."

Devora shook her head. Her mind wouldn't stop playing these tricks.

"You must trust me."

Charging away, Devora bounded through the trash instead of carefully picking her way along. She had to escape her own imagination.

"I won't ever leave you," Solange continued relentlessly.

The words faded away as Devora suddenly screamed in pain. She stared down at her toe in horror, watching as blood spilled onto the ground.

Wounds didn't heal in the Heaps. They usually became fiery mounds of pus and injured Heapdwellers would collapse in a feverish state. When they finally stopped muttering, the guards hauled them away—eventually. First, though, the gulls pecked their eyes and flesh as the rotting smell pierced the air. It was hard to believe that anything could add to the stench of the Heaps, but death could.

"I stepped on that glass because of you!" Devora accused.

"Shh," Solange whispered, touching the girl's forehead.

Devora sighed and her thoughts blurred as she drifted off into a welcome rest.

By the time she awoke, the noonday sun had thawed her chilled bones and her muscles had turned to soft gel. Her mirage of peace quickly fled as panic tore through her and she grabbed for her foot.

"It's fine!" she whispered, rocking and holding back tears as she caressed her unharmed foot. All five toes were perfectly intact. "It must have been all a dream—Jaron leaving, Solange appearing, my toe bleeding …"

Devora sighed and stood up. Then, remembering that she wanted to be ready when her name was called to leave, she spun around and narrowly missed stepping on one of the newly dumped Five-Years.

"She mended your toe," the girl said matter-of-factly.

Devora glanced around, checking for guards before replying crossly, "What are you talking about?"

"The Light Lady. She mended your toe. She stuck it back on while you slept. And then you didn't wake up until the sun grew tall in the sky."

"You're a liar," Devora hissed. It was all a dream. It had to have been a dream. If not, then Jaron was gone.

"Mama told me not to lie," the Five-Year said, looking like she was about to start blubbering.

Devora inspected the ground and discovered a crusted circle of dried blood.

Her blood.

She held her stomach. First, Benjamin was taken away, and now, Jaron really was gone. This stupid, snivelling Five-Year had turned her life upside down by telling her that her dream hadn't been a dream after all.

"You were not chosen! Your mama threw you away," Devora said between clenched teeth. She enjoyed watching the wretched little Five-Year crumple into a sobbing bump in the pile of refuse.

So the Five-Year saw this Solange too, she thought as she plodded away. That part hadn't been a dream either.

Trust. She mulled over the word Solange had used. She didn't know what it meant, but she did know that from now on Jaron and Benjamin were dead to her. They weren't strong enough to survive until Leaving Day.

She was.

She collected her things: a tattered skirt, her treasured pair of unopened cans of soda, a knife sharpened into a small but deadly point, and her favourite of Jaron's books, the red one. She stuffed everything into Jaron's sack with his newspaper clippings.

"You're ready. That's good."

Startled, Devora whirled around to see Solange. "You scared me!"

"Did you think I would let you face Leaving Day all on your own?"

Devora wasn't sure what answer Solange wanted to hear so she stayed silent, clutching the bag.

"I see you still don't trust me."

"I do," Devora hurried to answer. "It's just that you didn't tell me when you would be back."

"I told you I would never leave you alone."

"But I couldn't see you," Devora insisted hotly. She felt like she was on the edge of giving up, letting go, hanging on—she wasn't sure which one.

"Seeing me or not seeing me makes no difference. I'm still here."

"Prove it," Devora demanded, thrusting the bag toward Solange. "What did I put in here? If you're really with me even when I can't see you, then you'll know what's inside."

Solange's expression was difficult to see as the blinding glow she cast about her made Devora squint.

"I see you have much to learn about trust, dear child." Solange lifted her hands. "There are five things inside the bag," she said, pointing to her left index finger with the right one. "The first is the only extra piece of clothing you own. The second and third are identical—two unopened cans of soda. A huge accomplishment on your part to have collected such a treasure."

Gulping, Devora waited, wondering if Solange knew how the soda had come into her possession.

Solange touched her fourth finger as she continued down the list. "Also, a sharpened blade, christened by blood."

Devora's stunned silence ended. "I have never hurt anyone with my knife!"

"Ah, yes, your 'just in case' weapon. No, Devora, up until now you have only used the knife on four-legged predators."

Devora shuddered. How did Solange know all this?

"But you crave vengeance."

"I don't know what you're talking about."

"Don't hide from the truth within you, Devora."

The speakers blared across the Garbage Heaps, "Leaving Day candidates report to the door immediately!"

"I have to go now."

Solange kept pace with her. "Your last item . . . is a book—a red book."

Scrambling over the Heaps, Devora kept her eyes fixed on the door to freedom. She heard only her own footsteps but sensed Solange's shadowing presence. A group of Fifteen-Years had gathered in front of the door, some clutching belongings, others empty-handed. Devora stared at them with disdain. They were not chosen. For that matter, neither was she—not until now, anyway. Not until Solange. She stood taller and slackened her grip on the sack.

With a "thunk" the door burst open and half a dozen guards pushed through, positioning themselves throughout the group.

"Move it," a guard ordered, prodding her in the back.

She stepped through the doorway and stopped, silently questioning. A light glowed beside her. "Yes, I'm still here."

Moving in unison with the other Heapdwellers, Devora entered a narrow tunnel. They arrived at a huge cement box with metal spouts spaced evenly around the cinderblock walls. The guards shoved each of them in front of a spout.

"Strip!" the tallest guard ordered, tearing at Devora's shirt.

She looked around the room and saw the others nervously removing their scant clothing.

Devora obeyed too, shivering as she stood naked in a room of about thirty other Heapdwellers. Scalding water laced with white suds poured out of the spouts. Screams filled the room and she jumped away from the fiery rain, crashing into someone's wet body.

"It's okay," Solange said, gently touching her shoulder and steering her back into the water.

Eyes closed, Devora allowed the cleansing water to pound at her skin, attacking her arms and legs until they throbbed. When she finally opened her eyes, she saw the guard who had torn her shirt staring at her. He smirked, looking her up and down.

"I won't let him hurt you," Solange promised.

The water stopped without warning and Devora held up her hands, seeing her amber skin for the first time in her memory. Suddenly a roar echoed through the room and great gusts of warm wind circulated, drying her skin. Her hair flew wildly around her face, no longer caked with years of mud. The wind stopped and she, along with the other Heapdwellers, muttered soft sounds of amazement as they ran their fingers over their raw, clean skin.

"Pick up your new clothing and get dressed," the guard ordered, passing out blue shirts and matching trousers.

Devora collected her clothing, avoiding the guard's stare.

"You're a pretty one," he muttered under his breath.

Clutching her garments, she raised her eyes as far as the guard's neck. "Where are my things?" she asked, trembling.

"Burned in the incinerator."

"You had no right," she spat out recklessly.

The guard's face hardened. "You've got that backwards, you stupid program failure. It's *you* who has no rights!"

Unable to take her eyes from the guard's neck, Devora tugged the shirt over her head and stepped into the trousers. She didn't care about her clothes, her book, or even about her two treasured cans of soda.

"Like what you see?" the guard asked.

She finally tore her eyes away. Her things were gone. There was nothing she could do. She longed for her knife, her 'just in case' weapon. For now she knew the truth. The vengeance inside of her was screaming to be loosed.

"I rescued your book," Solange whispered.

Devora wished Solange had rescued the knife as well. She clenched her fists, locked in her daydream of slitting the guard's throat and revelling at the thought of his blood spewing onto the cement floor.

4

Out of the Fire

Jaron scratched at his bald scalp. He'd slept in a bed. A *real* bed. With a pillow, blanket, and mattress—all crisp and white. In a room, with something called a "light switch." It could be day or night with a flick of his finger.

He felt a prickle and dug at his right leg. The scratching must be from habit, as he couldn't possibly still be sharing his chafed skin with any other living creature. He'd checked. No bugs scurried in the seams of the mattress, and last night in the cinderblock room he'd been disinfected and stripped, disinfected and shaved, then disinfected and redressed in stiff khaki pants and a matching shirt. All material evidence of the Heaps was a blurred memory—except his key.

The water had scorched his skin, melting away the filth of ten year-spans. When he had stood at last, naked, the guard pointed to the key hanging from Jaron's tattered string.

"All scavenged trash from the Heaps must be thrown in there for burning," the guard said, nodding at the mound of discarded rags in a metal bin.

"It's not from the Heaps. It's ... it's from ... I had it before I came here," Jaron said, gripping the key and not caring that his bare skin was exposed. His only concern had been for the key—the faint reminder of his mother.

25

"Are you sure?" the guard asked, his gaze intent.

Jaron nodded, holding his breath, wondering why the guard's voice had lowered into a sharp whisper.

"Hide it! Don't let anyone know you have it," the guard had said.

Now, hours later, Jaron stared down at his trousers. They were a bit rumpled from sleeping in them, but the clothing was still the cleanest he'd ever worn. He sniffed at his hands and his stomach growled. *Mouldy carrots.* The smell of the disinfectant reminded him of scavenged food. It also reminded him that he hadn't eaten in ages.

The door to his room opened and the guard who had given last night's strange warning about his key now reappeared holding a tray. "Here, eat something."

Jaron stared at the feast. "It's ... it's first-day food. I've never . . . it's beautiful." Slices of crisp bacon curled temptingly next to perfectly cooked eggs on a spotless plate. Two stacks of toast framed the bacon and eggs like floppy ears alongside a grinning face. He crammed the food into his mouth and gulped the tangy sweet juice from the frosty glass.

The guard vanished and then returned a few moments later holding a chain. "You need to wear this around your neck," he said.

Jaron slipped it over his head. Cadet L754, not his name, was stamped on the tag. He let it drop to the outside of his shirt, keeping his key safely tucked underneath. "What happens—"

"This way," the guard interrupted, pointing to a tunnel.

Jaron felt smothered, like he was burrowing through a pile of trash. Even though the tunnel was free of debris, he felt buried underneath. He was used to the open sky overhead. What if the structure came crashing down around him?

He stuck his hand up to protect his head just in case.

"Arms by your side," the guard commanded.

They emerged from the tunnel and entered a wide-open space. Jaron stared. Ground. Flat ground. Clean ground. Uniformed people marching.

"Into the truck," the guard ordered, pushing him toward a large metal vehicle with all of its parts still intact.

Glass windows. Flawless metal. Jaron's hand brushed the smooth green surface of the "truck." He'd seen pieces of vehicles end up in the Heaps—some of the Heapdwellers even used the better ones as shelters. But he'd never seen a perfect one, like this.

The guard slammed the door shut and Jaron sat enclosed, his heart pounding. He'd managed to pull his foot inside just in time to avoid it being trapped in the door. Since he'd never worn any foot coverings before, the heavy boots made his feet feel like they were bolted down.

The guard opened the opposite door and threw a heavy canvas pack into the back before sliding onto the seat behind a small wheel.

"What?" Jaron gasped as the truck rattled and sputtered.

"We're going to the barracks. Just sit back and hang on." With that, the guard pulled on a stick and the truck jolted forward.

Jaron gripped a handle on the door as the truck flew along beside a cinderblock wall. Were the Garbage Heaps on the other side? Trees whipped by at a dizzying pace. He didn't know they had long, thick sticks at the bottom. All that had popped into view inside the walls of the Heaps were their leafy tops.

When the guard adjusted his hands on the wheel and the truck swerved in response, Jaron wondered if it was alive. As if reading Jaron's thoughts, the guard said, "It runs on 350 horsepower from the engine."

"Where are the horses?" Jaron asked, straining to look ahead and find the large creatures he recalled from the viewing screen at the morning message.

The guard chuckled.

Jaron sealed his lips together, determined not to ask any more questions. He might have grown up in the Heaps but he wasn't a stupid rat brain. He'd collected every scrap of newspaper and soggy book he could get his hands on. He had read of an outside world, but he had never been sure if it was real or not—until yesterday.

"The engine runs on fuel. The power it produces equals the power of 350 horses."

"Oh," Jaron mumbled, surprised by the warm tone in the guard's voice. "What happens to me now?" he ventured.

"I'm not supposed to tell the recruits," the guard replied with a quick glance in Jaron's direction.

"Tell me something. Anything!" Jaron pleaded. There was a kindness in this guard's face that made him willing to ask again—even at the risk of facing disappointment or possibly punishment.

Continuing silently, the guard manoeuvred the truck along the smooth winding trail. "I've been waiting for you," he said finally. "But I was hoping you'd make it until your Leaving Day. I was hoping you wouldn't pass the Heaps program."

Jaron blinked, staring out the window. *What was the guard talking about? Why had he been waiting? Who was he?*

The truck rumbled onto a narrow bridge, the wheels clanking against the uneven metal grates that planked the surface. Halfway across, the guard braked. "Something isn't right," he muttered. Jamming the stick in reverse, he revved the engine and the wheels spun, filling the air with smoke.

"What are you doing?" Jaron gasped as the truck flew backwards.

Drops of sweat beaded on the guard's brow. "We have to get off the bridge. Now!"

The rear wheels of the truck clawed at the dirt surface of the road just as a loud crack rippled, followed by an eruption of smoke and fire.

"Hold on," the guard yelled, twisting the steering wheel.

Jaron braced one arm against the dashboard and clutched at the door handle with the other as the front end of the vehicle flew toward the sky.

It's over, Jaron thought as the world tumbled around him. *I'm as dead as if I'd starved in the Heaps.*

The engine screamed and Jaron shut his eyes. "Devora," he whispered. With a guilty twinge, he realized he hadn't thought of her once—not even this morning when he'd gorged on first-day food after sleeping in silent luxury. He wondered whether she'd found something to fill her hungry belly this morning. Was she safe? Did she miss him?

He was jolted from his thoughts when the wheels hit earth and the truck catapulted over and over. Currents of pain shot down his neck as he tumbled inside the truck like a rat being flung by its tail. Then all was still, except for the sticky fluid that trailed down his brow and stung his eye.

"Get out!" the guard ordered, shaking him. "The fuel is leaking. Get out!"

Jaron was content to stay there, at rest, even as in the background the rank fumes of gasoline intensified. He felt the guard reach across him to pull on the door handle. Then he shoved Jaron out into the open to bounce through the grass, rolling away from the fuel that snaked along as if it was chasing him.

A deafening blast filled the air. Engulfed in flames, the truck crackled and chunks of metal glowed like fiery eyes on a cornered rat. The stench of burning fuel permeated the air.

Jaron stared, longing to be back within the safety of the Heaps, enclosed by cinderblocks, where the outside world was only a dream. He reached for his key and exhaled when he discovered that his one and only treasure was still fastened securely around his neck.

"Are you alright?" the guard asked.

"I don't know," Jaron said, squeezing his eyes shut, hoping that the world would stop spinning.

"You know, this happened because of what you did," the guard said, calmly standing up.

"What do you mean, what I did?" Jaron said, his anger feeding his attempt to stand in spite of his dizziness.

"You altered your fate by your choice."

"My choice? I've never had a choice!" Jaron could feel his rage consuming him, much like the flames that devoured the truck. "I was not chosen, remember?" he spat out for good measure.

"*He* wanted you to pass."

"What are you talking about?"

"By choosing to leave the Heaps before Leaving Day, you've played right into *his* hands."

Jaron tried to make sense of the guard's words as he rubbed his bruised head. "Are you saying that something I did *caused* this explosion?"

"No," the guard replied. "It was set by those who will blame the act on the innocent. But if *you* had made it until Leaving Day, your own path would have been different, easier."

Easier. Wistfully, Jaron craved a path that was easier than the one he'd travelled until now.

"Are you too injured to walk?" the guard asked. "We have a great distance to cover." He swung his heavy pack onto his shoulder.

Jaron wondered how he'd managed to retrieve it from the wreckage. "I'm fine," he snapped, wishing his head would stop throbbing. He took a few steps and then grabbed at his churning stomach.

"We'll rest here for another moment."

Jaron nodded and then vomited all over his new boots.

It took Jaron all afternoon, trudging behind the guard, to figure out what was different. He had weeded out the obvious— the trees, the grass, the beauty. But it wasn't until they had stopped to eat and the guard had started a small fire to make "coffee" that Jaron understood. He could smell. Everything. And everything carried its own unique scent. The burning wood. The boiling coffee. His own sweat.

Thankfully, Jaron had washed off the sour odour of vomit from his boots at the river not far from where they had crashed.

"Here you are," the guard said, passing him a tin cup filled with a steaming brown liquid.

Sniffing at the brew, Jaron ventured a tentative sip. "Ouch!" he exclaimed, jerking the cup away and dumping the contents over his trousers. "Dirty rat!" he yelled, jumping up and shaking off the offending liquid. The heat seared his skin and he felt tiny painful bumps swell on his tongue.

"Oh, right, you're not used to eating anything hot. Sorry."

Jaron frowned but said nothing. The guard had been teaching him mini lessons about their surroundings all afternoon as they trekked along the river. Pictures of animals such as sheep, deer, and skunks had flashed across the screen at morning message, but Jaron had never seen any real ones—at least not since he arrived at the Heaps just after his fifth birthday. And the ten year-spans he'd been there since had wiped away most memories of life before that.

"I have some extra trousers in my pack."

Again, Jaron marvelled at this mysterious "pack" that contained all sorts of useful things like tin mugs, a whole sack of sugar, and now, an extra piece of clothing. "How did you do it?"

"Do what?"

"Your pack. How did you pull it from the wreck?"

"I didn't," replied the guard as he dowsed the fire.

Watching the clear water being wasted in such a way made Jaron's heart skip a beat. He thought of thirsty Five-Years at the Heaps and wished he could bring them just one cupful.

"The pack was thrown from our truck. I found it while you were resting after the crash."

It was a small thing—a nagging feeling, a tug in his gut that had settled in to stay. Living in the Heaps with the "one for one" rule hadn't given Jaron much opportunity to learn about interacting with others, but this was instinctive. They had been chatting all afternoon with the guard looking him in the eye and promptly answering questions.

This time it was different. A pause. Eyes diverted. The guard was hiding something.

"What about the bridge?" Jaron tried again. "How did you know it wasn't safe?"

"No one manning the tower on the other side. Day or night, there's always someone on patrol."

"That's it?" Jaron said. "And from that you figured out we were going to be blown to bits?"

"Something like that," the guard replied evasively.

Another door slammed shut, Jaron thought. He stared at the trees bordering the water and imagined a snug shelter tucked away within the grove. A shelter for one, perhaps two, if he could ever find Devora again. "What happens next?" he asked, deciding to try another topic.

"The footbridge is around the next bend. We'll cross the river and arrive at the barracks by dawn. It may be for the best that the crash has given us some extra time."

"Time for what? You say that like the crash was something to be thankful for. We almost died!"

"There are things I must tell you. Things that will save your life."

"Are you saying someone is trying to kill me?" Jaron asked, his voice shaking.

"I'm saying if *he* finds you *he* will kill you, slowly. So slowly, that your body will become like the walking dead—a breathing empty shell."

"Who?" Jaron demanded.

"The enemy," the guard said, looking Jaron directly in the eye again.

"And who are you? Why should I believe anything you say? Guards are the only enemies I know."

"I am Ansel, a friend."

Jaron stared at the guard's face, weighing the word.

Friend.

"I know this isn't easy for you, Jaron. But if you listen to what I say, it has the power to save you." He collected the tin cups, stuffing them into his pack along with the coffee pot. "We should go now."

Jaron nodded, silently bidding goodbye to the grove of trees as he followed Ansel. Clasping his key, he wondered whether he was moving closer to, or further away from, finding a home.

"Why can't I just run away? Hide?" he asked.

Ansel flung out his arm and Jaron held his breath, preparing to be struck—an automatic response learned in the Heaps.

"This is the path you've chosen," Ansel said, patting Jaron on the shoulder instead. "What has begun must now be completed."

Breathing out, Jaron tugged at his key. It was a comfort to him, a habit.

Again, it was as if Ansel read his thoughts. "What do you know about that?"

Dropping the key with a dull *thunk* onto his chest, Jaron answered. "Not much, except it's the only thing that ever really belonged to me, even before the Heaps."

"Has anyone ever tried to take it from you?"

Shaking his head "no," Jaron attempted to swallow the acid taste that had crept into his mouth.

"Your enemy will try one day. I'll help when I can, but in the end you must choose your own path," Ansel said.

"My path? What does *that* have to do with my key?" Jaron asked.

"The path set out by the Ancient Way. It unlocks the door to home."

A path, a key, and now a door. Jaron puzzled over Ansel's mysterious words as the daylight faded and the moon blazed into the sky. "Tell me about the Ancient Way," he said, his voice cracking as he latched onto the words that breathed of something familiar. *A woman singing garbled words while brushing a girl's long golden hair. He was eating a cookie—watching, smiling.* His heart beat furiously and a chill from the night air crept over him.

"It's a path few have sought out. It's a belief long forgotten by most."

"I've never heard of it," Jaron said. But in his memory, the woman's melody grew louder and the voice, stronger. " Maybe my mother knew of it. Does my key have to do with the Ancient Way?"

"Something like that," Ansel said.

Why couldn't Ansel just tell him? Jaron gritted his teeth. His entire existence was a web of mysteries woven with Holding Shells, guards, and secret friends.

"The story of the Ancient Way begins with the beginning of everything, including the Realm of Leviathon and the land beyond."

Jaron held his breath. *There was a land beyond?*

Ansel smiled. "I see I have your attention now. But it's a tricky balance, Jaron, deciding how much to tell you. Some things I think you will have to find out for yourself before you will believe the truth. One thing you must remember, though, is that the enemy's power does not extend past the boundaries of Leviathon."

More riddles! Jaron thought, struggling to catch up to Ansel's quick stride.

5

The Other Side

"Name?"

"Freesia."

"Age?"

"Fifteen."

"Any history of medical problems?"

"No."

"Sign by the 'X.'"

Freesia chewed on the top of the pen, wondering if she should read the paper over first before she signed. She glanced around the reception room, choking on the odour of ammonia. Tracks of bare bulbs lined the ceiling, highlighting the rows of lily-white chairs stretched along azure walls.

"Sign!" the Matron said, tapping the "X" a second time.

As Freesia scratched the pen along the paper, she tried to read the smallest print at the bottom. She noticed the words "the undersigned shall herby revoke all—" just before the Matron whisked the paper away.

"Put this on," the Matron instructed, giving Freesia a crisp linen gown.

"But I've already had an exam."

The Matron sighed and shook her head. "And they say they pick the brightest and the best for the Maternity Program," she grumbled, directing Freesia to a row of changing cubicles.

Emerging from the cubicle, Freesia padded down the hallway in her sock feet and starched gown, following the soft swish-squash of the Matron's rubber-soled shoes on the marble tiles. No matter how hard she tried, she couldn't rub away the goose bumps on her flesh.

"This way," the Matron instructed, punching in a code on the alarm keypad.

Freesia stepped forward as the two steel doors slid open, revealing another narrow hallway lined with numbered doors.

"Wait in here," said the Matron, swinging open one of the doors to reveal an examination room.

A gurney covered in rumpled sheets loomed in the center of the room.

Blood. There was blood.

Freesia gagged.

"Leave now!" ordered the Matron, shoving her into the hallway.

Shaking, Freesia tried to think of something—anything—to erase the image burned into her brain. Mama, Papa, the farm ... anything!

Squelching a wave of nausea, her knees gave way as she sank down onto the floor. She began to count backwards, a trick she used to keep her mind from thinking of the rattlesnakes coiled in the wheat fields during harvest-time.

One hundred, ninety-nine, ninety-eight ... what had happened in there? ... *ninety-seven, ninety-six* ... they'd promised her parents she'd be treated like royalty ... *ninety-five, ninety-four*—

It was no use. Seizing her stomach, she buried her face in her knees, knowing she couldn't focus on anything long enough to strip away the memory of the scarlet stain that had spilled over the edge of the sheets and splashed onto floor.

She heard far away footsteps.

Then footsteps moving closer.

She lifted her head.

"Hello there, I'm Dr. Lyson. And you are…?" he said, waiting.

"Freesia," she finally whispered, surprised the words pushed through her lips forcefully enough to make a sound. She rose on rubbery knees and smoothed out her gown.

"Well, Freesia, why are you looking so lost?" he asked as he flipped through the papers on his clipboard. "I believe this is your intake room, right?"

The Matron burst out through the door, carrying a canvas sack laced tight with a drawstring. "It's ready!"

"What's going on?" Dr. Lyson asked sharply.

"Housekeeping detail is becoming sloppy. Program failures are most unreliable." With that, she marched away.

Dr. Lyson held the door open. "Please go in."

Soft music played and the scent of lilies wafted delicately from inside. Fresh linens were draped neatly across the gurney.

Freesia closed her eyes.

"What's wrong?" Dr. Lyson asked, his voice strong, yet comforting.

"There was blood."

"Don't worry," he said, and taking her by the hand, he led her into the room.

6

Benjamin's Revenge

Jaron tripped, swerving to avoid the steel blade. Landing flat on his back, he waited helplessly as Benjamin towered over him with both hands gripping the handle of the down-turned sword. The lethal edge of the blade pressed against Jaron's jugular.

"One for one!" Benjamin hollered. The whites of his eyes were bloodshot and his pupils dilated.

"Enough, Cadet!" the trainer said, levelling a gun at Benjamin and gesturing for him to move aside. "Remember, Enforcers fight the enemies of Lord Drake, not one another. Our training session is over."

Benjamin threw the sword and it landed with a thud in the sawdust.

Taking advantage of this reprieve, Jaron leapt to his feet and returned to his room. He welcomed the time to change into fresh clothing before the noon meal. It hadn't taken long for his stomach to grow accustomed to the hearty repast offered three times a day at the mess hall. When he had first arrived at the barracks, he had gaped at the mound of first-day food offered, sure that his stomach could never hold it all.

"One more scoop of potatoes," he said to the server behind the counter.

"Worked up an appetite today?"

"Yeah. Something like that," Jaron replied. He sat away from the others, the Enforcers. It made him sick to watch them eat— tearing the undercooked flesh from the bones, staining their teeth with fresh blood.

They all looked the same too, with their shaved heads and muscular bodies—like bald gorillas. He knew their bulked up frames were only partially due to the constant training and high-calorie diet.

Before Ansel had left him at the barracks six weeks ago, he had told Jaron about the injections and pills used as supplements. "The injections will be impossible to avoid. The doctor maintains scrupulous records. The pills are easier. Dispose of as many as you can."

By now, Jaron had pretended to swallow dozens of tablets, palming them until he could visit the latrine. The one time he'd had no choice but to take them he'd been so wired afterward that he couldn't sleep the entire night. He'd been in the gym until dawn, pounding the heavy bag and racing on the treadmill. At the following morning's training session, his blurry eyes and aching body cried for more of the drug. It was sheer will, and his faith in Ansel's warning, that had kept him from downing the next dose.

He sighed, wondering when Ansel might return. He'd promised Jaron he'd come back another time.

Benjamin approached Jaron's table and flung his food tray down. "So you still have that useless Five-Year trinket."

"What are you talking about?" Jaron asked. His stomach felt cinched in knots. *Why did Benjamin care about his key?*

"Your stupid key. You've kept it all these years. Why?"

"None of your business!" Jaron said. He remembered Ansel's question. *Has anyone ever asked you about your key?*

Benjamin shrugged as if he'd lost interest. "I went on my first Eradication last night," he bragged.

Jaron stayed silent and kept eating. Since arriving at the barracks, he'd been careful not to antagonize Benjamin's palpable hostility.

"Of course, I wasn't alone. After all, I'm still a Cadet," Benjamin said as he tore off a strip of meat and barely chewed before swallowing. He stared past Jaron as if he was invisible. "She didn't know what hit her."

Jaron gnawed harder on his food and breathed as loud as he dared. Anything to drown out the sound of Benjamin's voice.

"Her neck snapped quicker than a rat's."

Jaron stopped chewing. "Eradication means you *killed* someone?"

"Yeah, but no one calls it that. Can you believe it? They let me, a Cadet, have the honour."

"Why?"

"It's part of the training, Jaron. We've been chosen to be Enforcers, remember?"

Jaron felt like he was trapped in a cage of animals. He was an idiot to think being an Enforcer was some sort of noble distinction. "No. I meant why *this* person? Who was she? What had she done?"

Hatred exploded across Benjamin's face. "Who cares? I was following orders."

Benjamin swallowed more supplements and finished gulping his food. By the time the eager Cadet stood to leave the table his wild-eyed look from earlier had returned. "We've got it made. We're at the top. At least I am. You still talk like a lousy program failure."

As Benjamin spat out his angry words, Jaron knew he meant to insult him—trying to inflict pain.

"Maybe I'll report you. Tell the trainer that you're a rat-faced traitor. Bet you'd be thrown out of the barracks."

Staring at Benjamin's distorted features, Jaron worried that his former friend would read his secret thoughts. He actually longed to leave.

Grinning knowingly, Benjamin said, "But that's not what you're afraid of, is it?"

"I don't know what you're talking about."

"That's it!" Benjamin said, almost giggling, his pills fully kicked in. "You're afraid of the *killing*."

"And you love it."

"You know what the Holding Shells did to us! Dumping us there when we were only five."

"How can you know for sure? It happened so long ago." Jaron had been told the truth on that long walk to the barracks with Ansel, but he had been cautioned to say nothing yet. It wasn't the Holding Shells who were to blame for their exile to the Heaps.

"It's a program, Benjamin, get it?" Jaron inferred without blatantly stating the truth. Lord Drake ran the Heaps program to raise boys into savages that could be transformed into killing machines. And the girls—the ones who passed, that is—Ansel said they entered another program. They were trained as Interrogators, experts at garnering information at any cost.

Jaron had realized from Ansel's words that, even if Devora had passed the Heaps program, the two of them would have been immediately separated.

"What I get is that my Holding Shell threw me out like I was trash and that's why she had to die last night."

"What?" Jaron said, his heart hammering against his chest as Benjamin's words finally registered.

"Shocked, are you? Forget about it. You'll have your turn too. All Cadets get to eradicate their mothers."

Jaron flashed back to that night in the Heaps just months ago, the night he knew he had to outwit Benjamin and steal his shelter. He realized that now he was surrounded by an entire barracks filled with "Benjamins" united in their lust for power and revenge.

Why hadn't Ansel warned him of *this*?

Lumbering away, Benjamin emitted a sandpapery laugh.

"One for one," Jaron whispered, not from habit but from a deep knowing that he now truly stood alone. Turning his back on the others, he concealed his face, afraid of the unshed tears that threatened to betray him. Tears for his mother, his Holding Shell—the woman he could barely remember and now had to kill.

7

Paradise

Freesia reclined on a chaise lounge in the atrium, sipping fresh lemonade sweetened with honey. A plate filled with sliced fruit and teacakes rested on the table beside her, awaiting her first inclination of hunger.

Another white-robed girl approached the chaise next to Freesia. "May I join you?" she asked.

"Please do. I'm Freesia."

"I'm Katriel, but call me 'Kat.' All my friends do and I miss them like crazy." Kat's rounded belly filled out her flowing white robe.

"How long have you been here?" Freesia asked.

"Almost nine months. Nine long, boring months. How about you?"

"Six weeks," Freesia replied. So far she had been delighted with her private room and the gourmet foods presented to her several times a day. It had been a welcome retreat from labouring in the fields on her parents' farm. "I can't believe you find it boring. I love it here," she continued, thinking back to that first terrifying day when she had arrived at the program. Was that only just a handful of weeks ago? With her days now filled with massages and spa treatments, she couldn't believe how wrong her first impressions had been.

"It's okay, I guess. I'm finding it hard to get comfortable now that I'm so close to my Birthing Day," Kat complained, adjusting her cumbersome robes. "And, there's only so much pampering one can bear," she added, making a face.

"I know what you mean," Freesia said, giggling as she plopped a juicy wedge of pineapple into her mouth.

Kat giggled too—a beautiful melodious sound. "When did you have your procedure?" she whispered.

Reaching to touch her flat abdomen, Freesia replied. "The day I arrived."

"That's not so bad, then," Kat said, tugging at the hem of her sleeve. "I had to recover from my extraction first."

"Extraction?"

"Oh, it's nothing. It's better not to speak of it," she said quickly.

"I see," Freesia said politely. This was the first friend she had made since entering the program, and although she was curious, she didn't want to spoil things by prying. "What did you do before coming into the program?"

Kat's face brightened. "I was a singer. The youngest ever to perform for Lord Drake at one of his New Moon banquets."

She stared at her new friend, awestruck. "You must have been terrified!"

Smiling, Kat replied, "Not really. He's nothing special. Just another fat man with stained teeth."

"I bet his breath stinks too," Freesia said, covering her mouth to hide her snickering.

"Mm-hmm," said Kat, nodding and clutching her own shaking belly.

"Girls!" barked a uniformed Matron, appearing as if from nowhere. "Settle down. Katriel is in no condition to be partaking in such a foolish display. Remember yourselves."

Kat crossed her eyes in disgust as the Matron waddled away. "See what I mean?" she said. "The last nine months have been like an eternity in here. If it wasn't for that dreamy Dr. Lyson, all of the girls would probably pack up and leave after the first day of being bossed around by the Head Matron and her clones."

"Oh," Freesia said, her face growing warm.

"I see you've noticed him too."

"Not really," Freesia insisted. "I have a boyfriend ... well, a friend anyway, back home. He's coming to see me on Visitor's Day."

Kat took a sip of guava juice. "Don't get your hopes up. There aren't any visitors here."

"But they told me to make a list and I put Riak's name on it—along with my parents, of course." Freesia remembered Riak's kiss good-bye, their first kiss. He'd begged her to stay at home and ignore the summons from Lord Drake's palace courier. As if she could have refused. What a disgrace that would have been for her hard-working parents!

"I had a boyfriend too, a *real* boyfriend," Kat said emphatically. "He hasn't been here once."

"But that doesn't mean ..."

"Look, Freesia, I've been here nine months. You've only been here six weeks. There are things you don't understand."

"At least your parents visit, right?"

Kat pointed to the wrought-iron gate barring the far exit of the atrium. "Visitor's Day is something they promise, but no one ever comes, *ever*."

Freesia felt sorry for Kat. She looked like a forlorn barn kitten that had just been pushed out of the litter.

"It's not just me, you know," Kat said, as if she understood the significance of Freesia's pitying glance. "It's all the girls. No one comes to see them either."

Impossible, Freesia thought. Her parents had promised to visit, and they would. *And hopefully Riak will be with them.* She imagined his sun-browned skin illuminated by his mischievous grin. He'd been her neighbour and her friend for as long as she could remember.

"My parents will be here. They promised," Freesia said.

Kat didn't respond. Glancing over, Freesia noticed that her eyes were shut. She smiled—at least her new friend was able to get some rest now.

Freesia closed her eyes as well and tried to enjoy the artificial breeze wafting through the greenery. The soothing lull of a fountain completed the air of relaxation. Everything here seemed perfect, like paradise.

The gates didn't open once. No one came in and no one went out. Freesia tried to tell herself that it was only her morning sickness that made her feel so wretched. Tired and pale, her self-pity was in danger of choking any remaining optimism she might have.

It was Visitor's Day and Kat had been right. No one came. Not to see her, not to see anyone.

A ward girl tapped softly on the door of her room before entering with a lunch tray filled with an array of nutritious foods designed to tempt even the most finicky prenatal appetite. Freesia barely glanced up, successfully ignoring the small intrusion until the scent of herbed egg salad awakened her nausea. Racing to her bathroom, she clutched at her angry stomach, retching.

"You alright, miss?" the ward girl asked from the doorway, looking terrified.

No, she wasn't alright! Why did they pick the most stupid girls to bring the food trays? Glaring at the scrawny-armed girl in a loose-fitting uniform, Freesia pointed to the monogrammed towel hanging by the sink. "Put some water on it and pass it to me!"

Retching again, Freesia clung to the edge of the toilet, feeling a desperate need to lie down before she passed out. The ward girl handed her a soaked towel.

"What's wrong with you?" Freesia managed to gasp before hunching over the toilet again. "Wring it out first!"

The ward girl stood there holding the towel, as if mesmerized by the dripping water.

"Give it to me!" Freesia ordered, pulling the wet cloth to her face. Its coolness revived her and she managed to stagger out of the bathroom and drop onto her bed. The ward girl still stared, open-mouthed, saying nothing.

"What's wrong, haven't you seen anyone throw up before?"

The girl nodded, putting one hand to her belly and covering her mouth with the other.

"Then what's the problem?" Freesia gritted her teeth.

"It's my first day."

"Oh." Flooded with remorse, Freesia remembered how frightened she'd been on her first day in the program.

"And I'm not supposed to talk to you," the girl continued, glancing over her shoulder toward the door.

"Who's going to know?"

The girl's voice shook as she whispered. "I can't go back."

Freesia felt her anger slip away as she noticed the deep worry lines etched in the girl's weathered face. They looked strangely out of place on someone so young. Freesia had kept her own skin milky white by keeping a straw hat perched on her blond curls and a thick layer of protective cream slathered on her face and arms when she helped in the fields.

"Go back where?"

The girl gagged and ran into the bathroom. From the sounds of things she vomited just as violently as Freesia had only moments before. She emerged wiping her face with the same towel Freesia had used.

"It figures!" the Matron roared, bursting into the room and wagging her finger in the ward girl's face. "You program failures are lazy good-for-nothings. You should have delivered all of those meal trays by now. Don't think this incident isn't going to be reported!"

The girl grabbed at her stomach again and lowered her eyes. She seemed to whither, curling into a shrunken lump.

Freesia propped herself up on her bed and squinted her eyes into an angry stare. It was something she'd seen Kat do behind the Matron's back at least a dozen times. She lifted her chin as she spoke. "She was helping me."

The Matron smirked. "You don't give the orders around here—I do."

Holding herself still, Freesia hoped her voice wouldn't shake as she challenged the Matron. "It seems to me that you and your staff scurry around all day serving me and all the others in this program. I wonder why that is?"

The Matron's eyes darted uncertainly and her lips formed a thin firm line.

Heartened by the change, Freesia continued, "This girl helped me when I almost passed out. Would you rather she'd left me lying in filth on the bathroom floor?"

The ward girl uncurled herself, standing straighter, but her eyes were still downcast.

"You may finish your task," the Matron ordered, swinging the door open and stomping away as loudly as her rubber-soled shoes would allow.

"Thank you," the ward girl whispered.

"Forget about it. But you had better get used to the sight of vomit around here if you want to keep the Matron off your back. If she catches you and your queasy stomach, she just might send you away." She regretted her words instantly as the girl bleached almost white under her leathered skin.

"That's not why I threw up," the girl protested. "I'm sick almost every morning, even before I left the Heaps."

"What are you talking about? What are the Heaps?"

"I can't say any more. They told me not to," she said, shaking her head. She rested her hand on her stomach. "Oh, there it is again! There's something wrong with me," she said as panic filled her voice. "I know it!"

Yawning, Freesia now wished the new girl would hurry up and leave so she could nap. But knowing that the Matron wouldn't give a moment's thought to helping a ward girl, she felt a twinge of pity. "What's the matter now?"

The girl gulped. "It's my stomach. It's moving, like there are butterflies inside. And I'm sick all the time. I try to eat but I vomit everything back up and my middle is starting to puff out a little. How can I be getting fatter when I'm keeping down less food than ever?"

Freesia placed her hand on the ward girl's rounding middle. "You're right! Your arms and legs are like sticks but your belly is bulging a little. And you're throwing up! Are you in the program? No, you can't be," Freesia said, answering her own question, "otherwise you'd be in your own room being waited on."

"What do you mean? What's wrong with me?" the ward girl asked, looking like she would jump at the sight of her own shadow. "Am ... am I dying?"

Laughing, Freesia said, "No, you're not dying. I think, maybe . . . I know, why don't you go see Dr. Lyson and have him examine you just to be sure?"

"No, I can't make the Matron angry again. I'm fine, really," the girl replied, dropping her arms to her side and smoothing out her baggy uniform to disguise the tiny bump. "I don't want to cause any trouble. I'm just eating better food than before. I need to go."

"But if you're pregnant, you can get into the program and the cranky old Matron will have to wait on you too."

The girl's eyes flickered in disbelief as her hand flew to her mouth. "Pregnant?"

Didn't the poor girl even have a clue? Hearing the squeak of the Matron's rubber-soled shoes moving toward them, Freesia said, "You'd better go now. I don't think I can talk the Matron out of reporting you a second time."

"Thank you," the girl nodded, pushing the delivery cart toward the door.

"Oh," Freesia called out. "What's your name?"

"Devora," the girl whispered, whisking herself away just as the Matron rounded the corner.

8
The Father

It hadn't taken Devora long to settle into her new routine. First, deliver food trays. Then, pick up food trays. Most importantly, talk to no one unless spoken to. After her run-in with the Matron on her first day, things had progressed smoothly—boringly so. Which suited her just fine. She welcomed the routine, for with it came a roof over her head, three meals a day, and a locked door at night. If only she didn't have one nagging worry: her rounding belly.

"I'm starting to look like the other girls here," she told Solange one night as she latched the bolt on her door.

Solange, who had been appearing in her room every evening after Devora had completed her chores, nodded. "Yes, you are gaining a little. Nothing like the well-fed girls here. Even so, it'll be hard for you to hide it soon."

"Why do I need to hide my belly? None of the others do."

"They're in the maternity program, Devora. You're not!"

"I'm sorry. I promise I won't ask any more stupid questions," Devora pleaded.

"Don't worry, child. Tonight you and I must have a long talk. There is much for me to tell you." Solange reclined on Devora's bed and patted the empty space beside her. "Come here. Sit with me."

Devora sat down tentatively on the bed, still unaccustomed to the soft mattress. Carefully she lifted her feet and stretched out beside Solange.

"I was there with you that night, almost six new moons ago in the Heaps when this child was conceived," Solange murmured, running her fingers through Devora's hair.

"I don't understand. What night? What does 'conceived' mean?"

Solange's fingers paused. "The night you were … hurt."

"Stop it!" Devora wailed, curling into a ball and pulling her hands to her ears. "I won't listen!" She rocked back and forth, pulling herself to the edge of the bed. She couldn't bear the thought of anyone touching her, not even Solange.

"Quiet! You'll bring the Matron. One glance at you in that snug nightgown and she'll figure out why you wear a loose-fitting uniform."

Her body still shaking, Devora buried her face into her pillow to smother her terrified sobs. What did Solange mean— she'd been there *that* night?

Finally able to speak, Devora said, "How could you have been there? It was dark, so dark, not even the moon shone." She stared at the beautiful woman she trusted. The light still glowed around Solange as brightly as it had the first day she'd appeared in the Heaps.

"I can be where I need to be and seen if I need to be seen, remember? The guards didn't see me with you on Leaving Day."

"How can you do that?"

"Magic," Solange replied simply.

Devora stared at Solange's pale, perfect face and the glow that surrounded her. "Like the fairies in the storybooks I found in the Heaps?" she asked.

Solange nodded. "Similar. But my *power* is real."

When Solange said the word "power" her face changed for a moment. It transformed so fleetingly that Devora told herself she had imagined the brief hardened expression. "But if you had the power to be there that night, why didn't you … why didn't you …" Devora paused, knowing her words would sound like an accusation.

"Why didn't I stop it?" Solange asked.

"Yes," she whispered, searching Solange's face for pity, or some sign of regret—anything that would right this agony. She felt as though her heart had been shattered.

This thing growing inside of her, this Squealing Bundle, was "conceived" under the blackened sky the night she stopped believing in Fairyland. It was one thing to have faced that night alone. But for Solange to have been there and done nothing…

"I couldn't do anything, child," Solange said, pausing as if searching for the right words. "The … evil … that night was too strong," she continued.

Devora shuddered. When Solange had appeared to her the first time on the morning of her Leaving Day, Devora's frozen heart had been fractured just enough to allow Solange's light to seep inside. She'd felt as though she was worth something to someone. She'd believed in fairies again. "I trusted you."

"And you still must, child, for we have much to discuss and a long path to travel together."

"He hurt me," Devora said, squeezing her eyes tight to push away the memory.

"Shhh. I'm with you now and my power is stronger."

"But …"

Solange gave Devora a little shake and said, "What's done is done. We must move forward." Then she put her arms around Devora and tugged her close.

Devora resisted at first but then relaxed into the hug. Solange was strong enough to protect her now—if only she could trust her again.

"You know," Solange said gently, "I could have kept the truth from you."

Devora hadn't thought of that. How terrible it must have been for Solange to witness the attack but be powerless to help. She hadn't yet confessed to Solange about the conversation with Freesia. She'd discovered during her six weeks of training to become a ward girl that things always seemed to run more smoothly when Solange made the plans. But tonight she felt that there should be nothing left unsaid between them. "Do you think I should see Dr. Lyson?"

"Ahh ... yes ... that silly Freesia's suggestion. I was waiting for you to bring it up."

Her heart lurched as Solange spoke. "You knew already?"

Solange patted the top of her head. "I'm with you all the time, even when you don't see me. When are you going to truly believe me, child?"

"I do! I swear," she replied, anxious to prove her allegiance.

"This is most important, Devora! No one else must learn about your pregnancy yet. The minute Dr. Lyson or the Matron find out about you, you'll be exiled, sent to the wilderness to fend for yourself. Program failures don't get second chances, you know."

"What am I going to do?" Devora whispered, hearing the frantic tone in her own voice. She couldn't survive alone. "I should have left the Heaps with Jaron. He promised he would always look after me and find us a home one day."

"And what would a Heapdweller know or care about finding a home?" Solange asked. "Did it have something to do with a red book?"

"I already told you he didn't have any other red books." Devora sighed. Solange's questions were always the same: the book, a book, the red book. Solange asked every time she appeared, but the only red book Devora knew about was the one Jaron gave her with the stories of Fairyland.

"Even Heapdwellers have dreams," Devora whispered, wishing she had one of her own. "Jaron talked about finding a home, one that had a door with a lock his key would open."

Solange's glow brightened as a grin stretched her face taut. "The first thing we must do is keep you safe, so no more conversations with any of the residents here, understood?"

Devora nodded.

"The second thing we must do is name who it was that hurt you that night in the Heaps."

"No! I can't ... remember."

"If I knew a way to help you recall his face without causing you pain, would you let me?"

"Why? You said what's done is done."

"It is true, you must focus on your future. But once you remember who did this, I can pass the word along to ... someone who will see to it that he's stopped."

"How?"

"We'll make sure he pays for his crime with his life."

Nothing else but the promise of her attacker's death would have convinced Devora to cooperate. It wasn't enough for the monster to be stopped from hurting someone else—she didn't waste a moment's thought on the safety of the other Heapdwellers. After all, where had they been when she had cried out for help in the darkness?

"I'll do it."

Solange retrieved a notebook and pencil from the desk. "I'll begin by placing you in a trance. It's like sleeping," she explained, passing the items to Devora. "In this place you'll be able to see the face of the person clearly so that you can draw it. When I snap my fingers, you will be fully awake, remembering nothing, but we will have the drawing."

Taking a deep breath, Devora relaxed on her bed, propped up against her pillows with the pencil in her hand. Barely a moment later, she stared into Solange's glowing face.

"Are we starting now?" she asked.

Solange threw her head back, laughing heartily. "Oh child, don't you see? You're done! And you've managed to produce the most splendid drawing. You really are quite a talented artist for a Heapdweller. You must have practiced."

The notepad pressed against Devora's legs.

"Now look at your work, child. It will help you to face your fears and move forward," Solange coaxed, smiling again.

Devora knew she must force herself to look. She lowered her head and steeled herself to gaze into the eyes of the anonymous evil that had stolen the very depths of her soul.

"Jaron!"

9

Standing Alone

"This dose increase should help," the doctor said at Jaron's weekly weigh-in. "How's your appetite been?"

"Normal," Jaron lied, tugging his shirt on over his head. Really, he'd been gorging on as much food as possible in an effort to gain weight at the same rate as the other Enforcer Cadets.

"I'll run tests for parasites, just in case. Between you and me, I don't know how any of you survive ten years under those deplorable conditions."

"A lot don't," Jaron said, his voice catching.

The doctor gave him a shrewd look. "How was it again that you got into the Enforcer program?" He flipped through the file. "Ah, yes, here it is: a 'psychotic episode with a blatant disregard for imposed structure.'"

"What does that mean?"

"Basically, you flipped out. I'll run those tests, but in the meantime . . ." The doctor opened his stainless steel desk and took out a black and silver electronic device. He gave concise instructions. "When you press this button the machine will record your voice, and this other button will play it back to you."

Amazed, Jaron experimented with the slender device. "That's not me!" he said, listening to a stranger's voice.

61

"Yes it is, Cadet. Use that to record everything you eat this week. Your weight is likely nothing to be concerned about. Cadets have dips in their gaining rate from time to time as their training increases. You're obviously taking the supplements or you'd never have gotten this far."

If the doctor only knew, Jaron thought. He consumed twice the amount of food the rest of the recruits ate just to keep up.

"Don't worry. We've got time to bulk you up. Captain Mar will pass you as an Enforcer."

Jaron tried not to show any reaction. "What happens if I don't pass?"

"No one's ever failed the Enforcer program before. Usually by the time Heapdwellers end up here they're two steps past crazy and itching to fight."

Jaron tucked the recorder into his shirt pocket. It slid in compactly, not even showing a telltale bump.

"Don't lose that. It's my personal property. And you probably shouldn't let anyone know you have it either. I'm not supposed to give Cadets unauthorized technology."

"Maybe I shouldn't take it, then," Jaron said, reaching into his pocket to give it back.

The doctor shook his head, staring at Jaron's file. "Take it. We'll get you sorted out soon enough." Muttering something else about needing to tell Jaron's trainer to make adjustments to his exercise regime, the doctor handed him a small plastic cup filled with pills. "I've increased your dose to the maximum," he said. "Any more will put too much strain on your heart."

"I'll just get some water," Jaron replied, trying to calm his rapid breathing. Until today's weigh in, he'd kept up with the doctor's expectations. Sooner or later the doctor would suspect he wasn't taking the supplements. Then what?

The doctor waved him away. "Fine. Just make sure you take them all."

He stared into the cup as he walked to the water dispenser. It was necessary to keep up the pretence because the doctor's hawk-eyed receptionist made sure each Cadet swallowed the supplements within her view. He "took" them two at a time, transferring the tablets to his left hand and dropping them into his pocket. "All gone," he said, holding up the empty cup for her to see.

"Next time I want you to show them to me in your mouth," she said, frowning.

"I'm taking them," Jaron growled, trying to act more like he was "two steps past crazy." Even if his muscles couldn't keep up, at least he could mimic the erratic emotional state of an Enforcer. "Why wouldn't I?"

She stared at his neck, not answering. "Where did you get that?" she whispered, the pitch in her voice changing.

Jaron reached up, angry with himself for forgetting to tuck the key under his shirt after his physical. "It's nothing! Someone gave it to me. And you didn't answer me. Why wouldn't I take the supplements?" he baited her, wishing she would stop her eager gaze at his fumbled attempt to hide the key from view.

"I don't know why you wouldn't," she answered slowly. "But let me tell you why you should." After glancing at the guard standing sentry at the door, she continued in a hushed voice. "I'm sure by now you've seen the others and how they get after they take their supplements."

"Of course," he said. "I'm just like the rest of them."

"If you say so," the nurse said. "But if you're not taking them, someone will soon notice that you're different. Your muscles won't grow and your eyes won't bulge." Under her breath she added, "And most dangerous of all, you'll still be able to reason right from wrong."

That night almost six new moons ago in the Heaps flashed across his memory. Yes, he still knew right from wrong.

The guard posted by the door turned and asked, "Everything in order, Gabria?"

"Yes, I'm giving the Cadet some more of the doctor's instructions for diet and exercise."

The guard turned back to the hallway and she continued, "It happened to someone else."

"But the doctor said no one has ever failed the Enforcer program."

"It was before he came here almost five years ago." Gabria brushed back a loose strand of hair. "I was a Fifteen-Year and new to my post as assistant to the previous doctor. After six weeks of training they stuck me in here with these animals. If it wasn't for the guards swarming around the place I'd have been scared out of my wits."

The guard spun around and stared at them again and Gabria hurried to finish her story. "There was one Cadet who was different. We were ... friends. You remind me of him. Anyway, one night he disappeared and the guards said he'd run away."

"How?" Jaron asked, his voice filling with excitement. Maybe he could leave before ever having to do the terrible things they were training him for.

"Don't you get it?" she hissed, growing angry. "He didn't get away—they killed him."

"But you can't know that, not for sure."

"I know! If he'd escaped, he'd have gotten word to me."

"But ..."

"His file is marked with a red 'X.'"

"So?"

"That's how they mark the files of the dead," she said, nodding briskly at him, indicating the discussion was over.

"I'm sorry," he said.

"Don't be sorry—just protect yourself. If you value your own life at all, take everything the doctor gives you and forget you were once human."

Her eagle-eyed expression returned and Jaron knew that she'd stepped back into her role, an "enforcer" of the doctor's orders. His one moment of hope faded as quickly as it had appeared. The nurse would not be helping him escape having to eradicate his mother.

He gulped his lunch down in the cafeteria and arrived at the gym for an afternoon training session, all the while wondering if anyone else had noticed his even temperament. He jumped on the treadmill to warm up.

Twenty minutes later his trainer approached. "You need to come with me."

Jaron began the gradual decline of speed on the machine.

"You don't have time for that—you need to come with me now!" the trainer said, pulling the kill switch on the machine.

Lurching forward, Jaron grabbed the bar for support as the machine came to a dead stop. "Yes sir," he said, wiping the sweat from his forehead with his arm.

The moment the words came out he knew they sounded wrong—too submissive, too agreeable. "What do you want? I'm in the middle of my workout," he yelled, stretching his eyelids open as much as he could.

The trainer spun around, "Shut up and follow me."

Jaron obeyed, following the trainer to a truck outside.

As they drove away from the barracks, the trainer suddenly became more communicative. "This isn't part of the official training for Cadets, so when—or maybe I should say 'if'—you make it back here tonight, you'll still have to pass your Eradication. Got it?"

"Got it," Jaron replied stiffly. So this wasn't his Eradication. Even so, he hadn't expected to be facing his own death so soon after Gabria's warning this morning.

The trainer continued to talk, not waiting for Jaron to respond. "Remember your hand-to-hand combat techniques. You're smaller but quick. I suppose you could do a little damage with your right hook. It depends on who they've picked to fight you, though. That new guy fights like he scratched his way out of the Heaps. Are you listening?"

His jaw clenched, Jaron nodded. So he had to fight someone. Would it be a fight to the death? Adrenaline coursed through him and his muscles tensed. He'd been training hard, but so far the fights with other Cadets had been closely monitored in case someone raged out of control.

"I can't decide whether to put my money on you or not," the trainer said.

"Too bad," Jaron said, sarcasm lacing his words. "After all, I only have to worry about being slaughtered."

A metal building marked with the words "Over-land Vehicle Warehouse" loomed into view. The trainer slammed on the brakes.

"Watch it," Jaron snapped, his agitation now genuine. He jumped from the truck and balled his hands into tense fists, mentally reviewing his combat training.

The trainer moved toward the warehouse. "Hurry up, Cadet!" he yelled.

Jaron forced himself to follow. Gabria's words echoed in his head—*protect yourself ... forget you were ever human*. He reached into his left pocket and sighed with relief. The pills were still there.

10
The Return

The locker room reeked of dried blood and layers of sweat. Jaron longed for a window or a vent—something to offer a gulp of fresh air.

"Remove your shirt," the trainer instructed. "You fight bare-chested."

Jaron obeyed, pulling his shirt over his head. "What do I wear on my feet?" he asked, folding his t-shirt automatically. He grimaced. As if the discipline demanded of him at the barracks mattered on the day of his death.

"Wear your boots. The steel toes will come in handy."

"What do I do now?"

"You wait. Oh, and I suppose you could do a warm-up, although I'm not sure what difference it'll make."

Jaron jogged on the spot. His Cadet tag and key twisted together, bouncing recklessly on his chest without his t-shirt to hold them down.

"Take those off," the trainer said, muttering something about Heapdwellers and their worthless trinkets.

A flash of a memory, like a picture on a viewing screen, blinked for an instant. A woman's face. *Don't ever lose the key,* the hazy image whispered from long ago as Jaron tugged the tangled symbols of his two identities up over his face. Now he felt naked.

He unlaced a boot and slipped the key into the toe. He'd hidden it there many times during his training. He tossed the Cadet tag on top of his folded shirt.

"Tell me why I'm here," he demanded, attempting to use the strength he'd heard in his voice earlier that day when he'd listened to the doctor's recorder.

"You're here to fight."

"I know that! But why here?" he said, and then he immediately thought of a more pressing question. "Are there any rules?"

"Just one. Whoever is alive at the end of the match is the winner."

He sucked in his breath, now fearful each rise and fall of his chest would be his last. "*Who* am I fighting?" he questioned, recalling the strengths of the other Enforcers and Cadets with whom he had trained alongside in the gym. He didn't stand a chance, not really.

"I guess it can't hurt to tell you now. You're fighting one of us. One of the guards."

That didn't make him feel any better. The guards worked eight-hour shifts: six hours on duty and two hours of combat training. He wasn't sure if they took supplements, but he assumed they must in order to maintain their muscular frames.

During his time at the barracks, he'd gathered that guards came from another program where they grew up in families with two parents, attending schools and eating healthy food. They were part of the "Chosen" and revelled in bragging about these contrasting circumstances as they "inspired" the Cadets to work harder, driving the former Heapdwellers further over the edge of reason as they calmly wielded mind-game strategies gleaned from military school.

"Why did you pick me for this match?" he demanded, knowing that he was one of the smaller Cadets. "Don't you want the loser to have a fighting chance?" He remembered the fat rat that used to nest near Devora's shelter. It would take on rats half its size and win. The fight wasn't even sporting as the smaller rats were overpowered almost instantly. Then one day another rat almost equal to it in size challenged it. The fat rat didn't even bother to put up a fight—it was over before it had started.

"I didn't pick you. *He* did."

They were still alone in the bloodstained room but Jaron didn't need to ask who *he* might be. He'd heard that tone used dozens of times since Ansel had first referred to *him* on their way to the barracks six weeks ago. "Will *he* be here too, watching?" Jaron asked.

The trainer opened the door of the sweltering locker room to expose a wide hallway ending with a set of double doors. Light seeped through the slit between the two doors and Jaron could hear the dull roar of a crowd.

"I expect so. His cheers usually drown out all the others when the deathblow occurs. I'm leaving to place my bet. When the doors open, you can walk into the ring," the trainer instructed, whistling as he strolled away down a side corridor.

Jaron moved as if to follow him and a guard edged into view. "There's no way to escape," the guard growled, placing both hands firmly on his gun. "Wait until the doors open."

Bits of sawdust spilled out from underneath the doors. He was to fight in a sawdust ring. That, at least, was familiar. The roar of the crowd grew louder. Drums pounded out a rhythm and clapping hands joined in.

Standing alone—always alone—Jaron retrieved a pill from his pocket and watched it roll to the center of his palm. One. Just a single insignificant disk could alter him, magnifying his strength and endurance while diminishing his fear. A handful might make him invincible.

His mouth already tasted sour. He imagined chewing the bitter pill with no water to choke back the fragments. His lone hope for survival rested in the palm of his hand.

"One for one," he said, raising his hand to his mouth.

"Jaron."

He froze. Lowering his hand from his mouth, he lifted his eyes and stared into the face of a friend—his only friend.

"Ansel! What are you doing here?"

The guard left the question unanswered. He fastened his gaze on Jaron's fist. "You've been taking them, then?"

Jaron dropped his hand down. "No ... well ... yes. Once, when I had no choice. And I was about to just now. Have you heard what they're making me do?" He searched Ansel's eyes for understanding.

"I'm here to help you. Do you believe me?"

"Yes. You spoke truth to me when no one else would."

"Then listen now. You'll be strong enough without these."

He tightened his grasp as he weighed Ansel's words. "You mean I'll find the strength to die?"

"No," Ansel replied. "Today you must find the strength to live. Swear to me that you will not show mercy. Swear that you will fight to the death."

"What?" Jaron's heart leapt. He couldn't believe what he'd heard. His time with Ansel had been the one bright moment of kindness in his life. And now Ansel wanted him to *kill* someone?

"Swear it!"

Jaron unclenched his hand. "I can't do it without these."

"Yes you can. And you *must* strike your opponent when the opportunity presents itself. Swear it."

The door swung open and the frenzied yelling of spectators grew to a deafening cry. Jaron inhaled a burst of air that was infused with the crowd's almost tangible thirst for brutality. He inhaled again and found a moment of stillness beyond his surroundings. He was no longer alone. Ansel was there.

He threw the pill into the sawdust. "I swear it!"

A horn blasted and Jaron entered the ring.

11
The Time to Tell

For the third night in a row, Solange did not appear. Devora paced around her room, hands on her belly. The Matron had taken a second puzzled look at Devora's stomach that afternoon and worry had eaten away at her ever since.

Out loud, she said, "I know I'm not alone ... right?"

No answer. Maybe Solange was testing her again. She sighed in frustration. How many times would she have to prove her loyalty?

She changed into her nightgown—it was an effort to tug it down over her stomach now. She'd have to try and find a new one soon; the nights were getting chilly. She smiled, almost laughing at her own stupidity. The weather no longer mattered now that she'd escaped the Heaps. *Unless I get found out and sent away like Solange warned,* she thought.

A lamp cast a soft glow as she crawled into bed. On her first night in her new room she'd turned off her light and had felt a suffocating panic. Solange had appeared instantly, her brilliant glow putting Devora's fears to rest. Since then, she had opted to keep her lamp on while she slept.

A loud crash pulled her from her dream—she'd been floating on a cloud eating eggs, shells and all.

She sat up, disoriented. Where were the stars, the night noises? She reached for her knife but only found a scratchy thick blanket. "Oh," she said with relief, placing her hand on her chest and purposefully slowing her breathing. She was in her new room, the door was locked, her lamp was … out?

The room was smothered in darkness. The curtains were closed, squelching even the pale illumination cast by the stars. The memory of that shameful Darkest Night in the Heaps burst into her thoughts and suddenly she knew she wasn't alone now. She sensed a presence but could hear nothing except the pounding of her own heart along with her ragged breath. She reached out her hand, expecting to make contact with human flesh. Nothing.

"Who's there?" she whispered, pulling her hand back and yanking her blanket up to her neck. Why hadn't she gotten a new knife? She handled dozens of them each day when serving food trays. It would have been easy to tuck one away unnoticed.

The presence moved closer. She wasn't sure how she knew. There was no sound or smell, not even a rustling of air.

She had felt safe here. That's why she'd forgotten all about getting a weapon to protect herself. She'd put her trust in a locked door … and Solange. Where was Solange?

"I'm not alone!" she said, imagining herself moving across her darkened room and flicking on the light switch.

She felt a chill sliding around her, like her window had opened. The presence was even closer now. She bolted for the light switch, wanting to scream but forcing her lips to stay closed. Snap! Light flooded the room. It was empty.

The lamp lay extinguished on the floor, its plug pulled from the outlet. She pushed it back in and then hurried to a second lamp and clicked it on too. Three bulbs glared now, all of them together beaming light to every surface of her tiny room.

She checked her door. It was still locked from the inside.

Returning to bed was not an option. She shoved a wooden chair in front of the bolted door and sat stiffly under the blaring lights until dawn, all the while longing for the familiar aura of Solange.

Freesia licked the dripping butter from her fingers. She'd forgotten how delicious warm toast could taste. Awakening on the morning of the New Moon and discovering that her nausea had vanished in the eighth week of her pregnancy was a welcome delight.

The ward girl bustled around, brushing imaginary bits of dust here and there, lingering longer than usual.

"Did you see the doctor?" Freesia ventured, wondering if the girl might want to talk. They had chatted only briefly a few times since their run-in with the Matron on Devora's first day.

Even today, the girl seemed to be propelled by the unseen presence of the Matron as she cast timid glances toward the door. "Would you like some herbal tea?" Devora responded.

It was maddening. For two weeks she couldn't get Devora to discuss anything except the food tray. "Why won't you talk to me? I'm only trying to help."

Devora glanced over her shoulder, muttering that "she" might be listening.

"No one's here," Freesia assured her, wondering why the girl always resembled a skittish lamb. Other ward girls didn't wear that haunted look—but then again, they weren't hiding a pregnancy.

"I need to stay out of trouble. Program failures from the Heaps don't get second chances."

"The Heaps?"

"I'm not allowed to talk to you. She'll be angry …"

"Look around you. The Matron's not here, is she?" Freesia added honey to her tea, tired of trying to be friendly to this paranoid girl who constantly mumbled to herself.

". . . but maybe Solange isn't listening anymore," Devora whispered.

She'd spoken so softly that Freesia wasn't sure she had heard correctly. Forcing all impatience from her tone, she tried a different approach. "I know something must be troubling you. You look like you haven't slept all night."

"I didn't."

"So have you gone to the doctor yet?"

"I'm not like you. You're in the maternity program. I'm not."

Freesia couldn't understand this girl at all. What was she so afraid of? People *were* civilized and everyone *was* treated kindly in Leviathon—except for criminals, of course. After all, Lord Drake had to make sure his Realm was safe. Surely Devora wasn't a criminal. "Does your family live nearby?"

"I have no family," Devora whispered. "I have no one except Solange, and she said not to tell anyone that I'm pregnant. But you've already figured that out," Devora mumbled, "so maybe …"

Freesia pushed aside her food tray and pointed to a chair. "Why don't you sit down for a minute?"

Perching obediently on the edge of the seat, Devora stared at the frosted window. "I spent years imagining what it was like within the White Palace and hating everyone inside for seeing us and doing nothing. And now I am as blind as you. Your windows are coated to let light in but you can't see out."

This girl spoke in riddles. They weren't in a palace. And the frosted glass simply gave privacy. *Maybe ward girls are mentally unbalanced*, Freesia thought, sliding protectively to the far edge of her bed. She'd been trying to help this half-starved girl, not thinking of her own safety or her baby's. What was it Devora had called herself? A program failure?

A siren blared and Freesia bolted off the bed, grabbing her wrap.

"What is it?" Devora shouted over the noise, jumping from her seat.

"Emergency drill," Freesia replied. "They have one the morning of every New Moon. Didn't the Matron tell you?" Not bothering to wait for an answer, she grabbed Devora's hand. "Come on!"

They joined the throng in the hallway, a mix of giggling maternity participants and solemn ward girls—together, yet separate.

"Where are we going?" Devora asked, her fingernails digging into Freesia's arm.

"It's just a drill so we gather in the atrium until the 'all clear' signal is given," Freesia answered as another stream of mothers cradling infants entered the flow. A little tot in front of them poked his head out from underneath his blanket and gave a toothless grin. "You're adorable!" Freesia cooed.

"A Squealing Bundle," Devora whispered, reaching out toward the infant's fuzzy head and then whipping her hand back. "I didn't know what they looked like."

"A baby?" Freesia gaped. "You've never seen a baby? Not even in a pram in Corwyn City?"

The ward girl gave a blank stare. "Only Five-Years come to the Heaps. And I don't know anything about Corwyn City except what's in Jaron's newspapers."

What were these "Heaps" she kept talking about? Freesia didn't understand how this girl could know so little about life in Leviathon. Where had she been all these years?

The Matron marshalled them into the atrium where the lush greenery and trickling water dulled the sounds of mothers' voices and whimpering babies.

"There's no open sky," Devora said, staring at the domed glass above the palms. "You can't hear or smell the Heaps either."

"Everything's monitored here. Even our air quality," Freesia said with pride creeping into her voice. "Scientists and doctors work together to keep our environment pure."

"Seems like a waste to me," Devora said, sneering. "Raising perfect babies only to throw them out in the garbage."

Placing her hand on her abdomen, Freesia shuddered. As soon as this drill was over she'd tell the Matron to assign a new ward girl to her room. The tranquil spell of the atrium was broken for her now with Devora's words.

The Matron suddenly shouted as the glass shattered on the southern side of the dome and a biting stench overwhelmed the atmosphere. "Everybody move in an orderly fashion. This is not a drill! We have to retreat to the lower level!"

"Do you smell that?" Devora hissed. "It's the Heaps!"

Mothers screamed. Babies cried. Pregnant girls hunched over with their arms around their middles as they were herded through another corridor and down a staircase.

"Where are we going?" Freesia cried.

"You'll survive," Devora answered sharply. "These are the stairs to the kitchen."

12

To the Death

Jaron stood alone in the centre of the ring, waiting for his opponent to show himself.

Lights glared down, blurring his vision. He saw dim shadows and smelled the stench of unwashed bodies. This, mixed with frenzied yelling, informed him that the room was crammed full with spectators eager to see him devoured.

Another set of doors burst open and a column of guards filed into the ring. The hair prickled at the back of his neck. The seconds seemed to stretch across the length of his lifetime.

Memories he'd forgotten flashed through his mind— moments of insignificance, yet they demanded his attention. *Eating an apple riddled with holes yet finding no worm. Digging a grave for his small companion—a rat, the runt of the litter.*

The guards faced each other as they divided into two rows. Standing at attention, the glassy-eyed husks of men cradled their guns to their chest.

A rustling noise alerted Jaron that the crowd was scrambling to its feet. An announcer entered the ring and spoke into a gilded megaphone. "Citizens of the Realm of Leviathon, raise your hand as you swear your allegiance to our Ruler."

Another rustling indicated the crowd's obedience. The announcer continued, "Say it with me. I swear by the New Moon that I will serve the Master of the Realm."

A drumbeat began, slow and steady, building into a dizzying rhythm as the crowd screeched and clapped. Abruptly, as if on cue, they stopped.

The announcer moved to the side of the ring and said, "Welcome your Leader, you loyal subjects of the Realm of Leviathon. Welcome Lord Drake."

In unison, the twelve guards twirled their guns overhead and then snapped them back into place.

The beads of sweat soaking Jaron's skin instantly transformed into pellets of ice. A chill had infused the room, reminding him of the relentless cold that had often seeped into his bones at the Heaps. The lights that had been focused so intensely on him when he'd entered the ring no longer seemed to radiate their oppressive heat.

He shivered, hating himself for showing weakness.

Lord Drake glided into the room wearing a hooded black and red cloak draped in folds around him, rippling as it brushed against the sawdust. Two guards stepped forward to remove the garment, revealing a man unremarkable in most of his appearance. The one exception was his eyes—they were translucent, almost vacant one moment and piercing like cold steel the next.

An armed guard broke rank and sidled next to Jaron, driving his gun into the back of his leg. "Cadets bow in the presence of Lord Drake," the guard hissed.

Gritting his teeth, Jaron bit back a cry of agony and lurched forward onto his hands and knees.

"Scrawny little thing, isn't he?" Lord Drake said, circling around Jaron's body.

Jaron kept his head down but could see Lord Drake's boots making a path of footprints in the sawdust. So the great leader of the Realm was mortal after all.

"Look at me!" Lord Drake commanded.

Jaron obeyed, squinting as the lights cast down an unrelenting glow.

Lord Drake brought his lips close to Jaron's ear. "Where is it?" he growled.

Jaron was too stunned to respond. What did he have that Lord Drake would want? He owned nothing.

"Never mind," Lord Drake said. "I'll have the guards search your dead body."

Jaron impulsively reached for his boot.

Lord Drake grinned, baring his stained teeth. "So that's where you've stashed the key, is it? You little garbage rat."

His key? How had Lord Drake found out about his key?

"There's something you should know before you die, you insignificant piece of trash," Lord Drake hissed. "The opponent you'll be fighting is your 'friend,' the one who betrayed your identity as a Holder of the Key."

It would be Benjamin, then. So this was it. He would fight his former friend and one of them would die. Anger swirled inside of him, building until he feared he would explode. That's why Ansel had made him swear to kill his opponent. Now he could finally unleash the vengeance he'd been unable to deliver before. He'd held back in the Heaps when he'd seen Benjamin skulking away from Devora's shelter. At the time, he'd been too cowardly to strike out.

Jaron replayed that night in his memory: the driving rain, Devora's terrified screams, him racing, tripping in the blackness, Benjamin running past him.

By the time Jaron had reached Devora's shelter a guard had appeared, so he'd stayed hidden. The next day, Devora's arms were bruised and she had a jagged cut above her lip. And her eyes were different, empty. When Jaron found a moment to ask her what had happened, she told him nothing. When he insisted, she only said, "I no longer believe in Fairyland."

Jaron had plotted while still in the Heaps, suspecting Benjamin but never confronting him. Despising himself for this failure, Jaron had compensated for it by positioning himself closer to Devora—stealing Benjamin's shelter.

Shaking his head, Jaron forced his focus back to the present as Lord Drake boomed, "Let the game begin!"

The Supreme Ruler moved to the edge of the ring and took his seat. His guards posted themselves around him, a living shield protecting him from his sworn loyal subjects.

Jaron rose to his feet, wincing as he tried putting weight on his battered leg. Ansel brushed by him and Jaron breathed a sigh of relief that his friend had not abandoned him in his last few moments of life. "Bury me under the trees near where we ate that day," he begged.

"You will not die," Ansel insisted.

The announcer quieted the crowd. "All betting is closed now," he shouted. "Fighters, take your place at the centre of the ring."

Ansel stepped out to face him and Jaron's blurred gaze finally took in that his friend no longer wore the shirt to his uniform.

"What...?" he said, then froze as the impact of his realization crushed his insides.

"Watch for your moment of opportunity," Ansel said, raising his fists.

It was unthinkable that Ansel could have been the one who betrayed him to Lord Drake.

"I thought you were my friend," Jaron said, choking on the words as if they were poison.

"And now you think differently?"

A blast from a trumpet quieted the crowd, giving Jaron no opportunity to respond.

"Begin!" shouted the announcer.

Ansel threw the first punch and the crowd hollered. Jaron countered with a blow that made Ansel stagger. Jaron tried not to show surprise. He knew the limited power behind his punch could not possibly have caused Ansel's dramatic reaction.

"So you've decided to play a stupid game with me first," Jaron said as he threw another punch. It had only taken him a second to realize that Ansel was the strongest and most skilled opponent he'd ever faced.

"I already told you, Jaron, your life can't end today."

Jaron lunged forward, kicking Ansel in the groin.

"It will be over in a moment," Ansel groaned. He fell to his knees.

"Stand up!" Jaron screamed. The cheering of the crowd fuelled his need for revenge.

Ansel staggered to his feet and grabbed Jaron's arm.

A glint of steel caught Jaron's eye and he ducked to avoid the blade of a knife. "So you don't fight fair after all," he accused.

"Why do you hate me?"

Fatigue seeped through Jaron's muscles. His disappointment in losing Ansel's friendship now outweighed his adrenalin. He knew that they were performing an elaborate show. A kick here, a punch there—nothing real except the knowledge that very soon one of them had to die. "Lord Drake told me that you betrayed me," he said.

"And you believed him?"

Jaron blinked. The moment in the Heaps when he'd chosen to pass the Enforcer program crashed into his thoughts. Only once in his life had he been given an opportunity to escape his fate. He hated himself. He hated his choice. He hated this world. He hated everyone and everything. But Ansel?

"Jaron, hear this. I did not betray you. So decide quickly if I am your friend or your enemy." He grabbed Jaron's hand again and made it appear as if they were struggling for the knife.

Horror filled Jaron as he realized that Ansel was turning the blade toward himself. "No!" he cried out, tripping. His arm plunged forward and the blade tore into Ansel's abdomen.

Sweat matted the guard's hair and the colour ebbed from his skin.

"I believe you are my friend," Jaron said, his eyes pleading for forgiveness.

"I am who you say I am," Ansel said, still clutching Jaron's hand.

Jaron's tears spilled and mixed with his sweat. "I'm sorry," he cried.

"I've taken your place," Ansel whispered and then slumped to the ground.

He stared as the blood seeped out from underneath Ansel's body. Ignoring the cheers and screams of the crowd, Jaron gently turned him over. The guard's lifeless eyes stared back as if they could see clear into Jaron's heart.

The announcer approached. "We have a winner! Retrieve the knife, Cadet. You've earned it! You can use it on your next mission."

Confusion coursed through him as the announcer's grim expectations waded through his shock. Once again, he stood alone. He gripped the knife with one hand and pressed against Ansel's chest with the other. The knife shredded his friend's flesh as the jagged edge resisted. Jaron cringed, feeling as though he was cutting himself.

The announcer reached down and grasped Jaron's quivering arm and shoved it into the air.

Gazing up, Jaron watched Ansel's blood drip down from the knife, covering his fingers.

Lord Drake strolled toward him, his eyes reverting to their glinted steel appearance. "You inflicted a wound motivated by revenge, Cadet. Now that key belongs to me!" he said, reaching out his hand.

Jaron wondered at the sudden stillness, startled by a comforting peace in the presence of his enemy. He unlaced his boot and withdrew the key. Had Lord Drake's hunger for this worthless trinket been the catalyst to Ansel's death? He held out the key, no longer caring about Ansel's warning. What did the counsel of a dead man matter now?

Lord Drake lunged for the key and then suddenly recoiled as if he'd been singed by an invisible flame. "It can't be!" he yelled, his eyes flashing.

Amazed, Jaron stood motionless, studying the key as it reflected a glimmer of light.

"Next time! I *will* have it!" Lord Drake snarled, stomping away.

A swarm of guards surged forward and Jaron stepped aside to let them bury their dead. Instead, they hoisted Jaron to their shoulders and carried him out of the ring. He tried to take one final look at Ansel, a last good-bye, but the doors slammed shut. He felt ill—insects gave more care to their fallen.

"Tonight we celebrate," his trainer cheered, racing to keep up with the crowd and patting Jaron on the back as if they were comrades. "Then you'll have a few days to rest up before your big test."

"What test?" Jaron asked, slipping the key back over his head and carefully hiding it away. *Why couldn't Lord Drake take the key from me?* he wondered.

"Relax, Cadet. You've proven yourself." The trainer grinned. It was clear he felt entirely responsible for Jaron's success in the ring.

"What's the test?" Jaron asked, certain he already knew the answer.

"It's simple compared to today. You'll do fine. The Eradication will be over before you know it."

Eradication.

So the killing wouldn't stop.

For this one brief moment, Jaron hated Ansel too. By taking his place in death, his friend had robbed him of the only means to escape his life.

13
Project Heaps

The radiance of the New Moon filtered through Freesia's window as she again enjoyed her new favourite snack, warm buttered toast. "That odour in the atrium after the glass broke was awful," she said, noticing the feeble shadow cast by Devora in the moonlight. After the day's events, she hadn't had the heart to ask the Matron to assign her a new ward girl.

"It came from the Heaps. I breathed it in every minute for ten year-spans," Devora said, glancing around the room. "I wish I'd been raised for this program instead!"

"I'm sure it wasn't too bad," Freesia said, thinking of her long hours of work on the farm. She hadn't lived in this luxury her whole life either.

"Wasn't bad?" Devora's eyes blazed as she stood up. "Have you ever eaten meat crawling with maggots or gone days with absolutely nothing to drink?"

Freesia's nausea finally returned full force. "You can't be serious," she said. "There isn't ... Leviathon isn't like that. There are programs—"

"Programs!" Devora spat out. "Let me tell you about *my* program. The Garbage Heaps. For ten year-spans I slept on garbage, ate garbage, *was* garbage!"

"Stop! Please."

"You're here, coddled and spoiled, and all the time you're just a Holding Shell for an experiment. I heard enough wisps of rumours to know that Five-Years started out here and ended there." Devora stood with her fists clenched and her shoulders shook as she spoke.

Freesia squeezed the down quilt on her bed, her insides twisted like coil springs. "No. You're wrong! The babies are trained to be doctors, scientists, teachers . . . it's part of Lord Drake's plan to strengthen Leviathon."

"I lived there until two new moons ago! Do you think I imagined the rats and the cold as I scrounged enough food just to stay alive? We were treated like animals, not even allowed to speak to one another or we'd be thrown out as failures."

The warmth of her mother's farmhouse kitchen flooded Freesia's thoughts. She couldn't imagine ten years of isolation and near starvation.

"But in the end I failed anyway," Devora continued. "It was a cruel joke. The ones who rebelled and broke the rules were valued and I was still the trash."

"But how could you survive without speaking to anyone?"

Devora slumped. "I had two secret friends, Benjamin and Jaron. At least I used to think they were my friends. Benjamin got taken away first, and then Jaron, just before our Leaving Day."

"You must miss them."

"No, I don't," she said. "They left me behind."

"Didn't they try to help you?"

"No one helps you in the Heaps." The angry fire sparked and then quickly died in Devora's eyes.

It was inconceivable to Freesia that such a program existed. She had been staring intently at Devora the entire time, wondering if the girl was capable of inventing such an extraordinary tale. Then an awful thought hit her. "What kind of mother would even permit her child to be dumped in the Garbage Heaps?" she asked.

"The Holding Shells," Devora said, her eyes burning with accusation. "The ones like you who are treated like queens and then forget the faces of their babies. They told us every day in the Heaps that we were the ones not chosen."

Curdled bits of warm buttered toast slid back up Freesia's throat and spilled down over her silk nightgown. It wasn't true. It couldn't be true. She couldn't have been brought here and given the finest of care only to be forced to discard her child like garbage. Her child would be something great—that's what Lord Drake promised participants of the maternity program. Her stomach tensed as she thought back to the paper she'd signed on her first day, wishing she'd insisted on more time to read it over.

"I don't believe you," she said finally, as if speaking the words out loud would make them ring true.

Devora stacked the dirty dishes in the bin at the bottom of her cart. "You think you're better than me," she said, throwing the butter knife in with a loud crash.

"That's not what I said."

"I heard it in your voice. You believe I'm no better than a rat, that I can't know something you don't."

"I just think I would have heard something before now. Maybe ... well, maybe your mothers just abandoned you and it has nothing at all to do with the maternity program."

Devora glared at her for a moment and then said, "Think what you want. I don't care about you or your wretched baby." Then she pointed at her own stomach. "I don't even care about this thing. I never asked for it and I'm not going to let it be the reason I'm sent away," she said, whirling around and shoving the cart in front of her.

Freesia slipped from her bed and washed her face, changing into a fresh robe. This day had started with confusion and broken glass, and now her thoughts continued to swirl in turmoil. Was there really such a horrible place beyond her sheltered haven?

The door burst open and the Matron bustled in, followed by Katriel pushing a lacy babycart.

"You have a visitor," the Matron declared needlessly.

"Visitors," Kat corrected. "I told the Matron we could announce ourselves, but she insisted that she check on you after the commotion today."

Anxious to speak with Kat alone, Freesia said, "I don't need anything right now. Please leave us."

The Matron marched away, complaining about "insolent ingrates who ignore curfews."

Kat giggled. "I see you've finally put her in her place."

Freesia tried to focus on Kat's new baby girl. "Let me see her. Where've they been hiding you both?"

"I've been in isolation recovering from my 'ordeal.' Then they moved us to a new wing, separate from the Maternity Ward."

"Was your Birthing Day difficult?" Freesia asked, peeking at the baby's delicate face.

"Not really. It was nothing like my mother had warned. She said I'd be in agony for hours, maybe even days. But the minute my water broke they injected me with sleeping medicine. And when I woke up, Scarlett had been born."

"What a pretty name! Did you get to chose it?"

Kat nodded. "Mm-hmm," she said, gently rocking the babycart. "I chose it from the list they gave me after I'd signed my new contract."

Freesia's thoughts catapulted back to her earlier worries. "What was the contract for?" she asked, her voice strained.

"Scarlett was assessed at birth and then assigned to a nurturing program. I agreed never to interfere in her development."

Freesia felt her knees weaken. "What happens if you do interfere?" she whispered, almost choking on the words.

"What a silly question," Kat said, laughing. "The nurturing program nurses are experts on childrearing. Why would I get in the way?"

"I don't know. But why do you have to sign a contract if everything's so wonderful?"

Kat's smile faded. "I don't know, Freesia. You're all worked up after today. I'll ring for your ward girl. You need a cup of herbal tea."

"Do you know what nurturing program Scarlett was assigned to?" Freesia asked, fear chewing at her insides.

"Let me think. It was something mysterious sounding. Oh yes, I remember—Project Heaps."

"That's all you know? You didn't ask any questions?" Freesia stared at the frosted window. Would Kat be a "Holding Shell," forced to dump her precious Scarlett one day?

"Freesia? Freesia!"

"What?"

"Your tea will be here in a minute. Would you like to hold Scarlett?"

She sat down in her rocking chair and Kat placed the tiny bundle into her arms.

"I can't wait until your Birthing Day," Kat said, tucking the pink blanket in around her baby.

Freesia bent forward and nestled her cheek into Scarlett's hair and inhaled the delicate scent of flowers. Soon she would have a baby engineered to be one of society's greatest contributors—a girl, Dr. Lyson had told her.

"We can raise our babies together and they'll be great friends, just like us."

Don't say it, Freesia thought, closing her eyes and clutching the baby.

"Oh! Maybe our babies will be in the same nurturing project! Wouldn't it be great if you got assigned to Project Heaps too?"

Devora entered the room, carrying a tea tray. Freesia gazed at the ward girl's worn face and then peered into Scarlett's innocent eyes. A revelation of truth blew in like a windstorm. "Never!" Freesia cried, thrusting Scarlett into Katriel's arms and racing from the room.

14
Hide and Seek, Find and Run

"You wicked girl!" the Matron scolded. "Stop your racing through the hallway this instant!"

Gripping the handle of her food cart, Devora paused. Now she'd never be able to catch up with Freesia.

"This is supposed to be a relaxing atmosphere!" the Matron screeched. "Do you think charging around clanging dishes is relaxing?"

A purple vein throbbed on the Matron's neck. Devora suspected that now might not be a good time to point out how much the Matron's shrieking ruined the "atmosphere."

"I had to—"

"She had to find you because my baby felt feverish," Katriel interrupted calmly from behind Devora.

"Well!" the Matron bristled. "You could have had me paged."

"I didn't think of that. If it's too much bother for you, I'll just go to Dr. Lyson's office and tell him you were too busy to tend to Scarlett."

The effect of Katriel's words left Devora breathless. The Matron busied herself feeling Scarlett's forehead and cheeks with the back of her hand. It was as if Devora had become invisible.

"That's all for now, ward girl," Katriel said, dismissing Devora with a nod that urged her to continue searching for Freesia.

Where would she go? Devora wondered. Walking as briskly as she dared, she made her way to the housekeeping wing and rode the sliding lift down to the kitchen. She hated being trapped in the moving cage, so after depositing her cart of dirty dishes she took the stairs back up to the main floor.

Not desiring to encounter the Matron's wrath again, she shuffled, with eyes cast down, back to the atrium.

The glass from today's mysterious incident had been swept clean and the hole in the dome sealed off. The fragrance wafting from the flowers gave an air of calm that her pounding heart couldn't mirror. The gagging smell from the Heaps was long gone, sucked away by the dome's efficient climate control device.

She bent forward to sniff in the delicate perfume from the lily of the valley's white bells dangling gracefully from fragile stems. The unspoiled blooms seemed unaware of their vulnerability. Gazing past the fountain, she saw Freesia huddled beside the barred exit door. She rushed over to her side. "I've been looking everywhere for you."

Freesia kept her head buried in her arms. "The doors are locked, every last one of them," she said, her voice muffled.

"You need to come back with me," Devora said, wishing she'd never said anything about the Heaps. What if the Matron found out what she'd done and sent her away?

"No one comes to visit. No one comes in. No one goes out. We're prisoners!" Freesia sobbed. "And there was the smell ..."

A few girls in the atrium glanced their way. "I'm going," Devora whispered, anxious to return to her room now that she knew Freesia was accounted for.

"Wait!" Freesia said.

Devora obeyed. Others were watching and she must be seen attending to Freesia's demands.

"I need your help," Freesia said.

"Fine, then. Get up and I'll take you back to your room."

Freesia had already jumped to her feet. "I don't need assistance walking. I need your help to leave this place."

Devora stood, her mouth gaping open. "You can't mean that!"

"I'm not taking a chance that my baby ends up like you did—abandoned and alone, scrounging for scraps to survive. I won't send her to the Heaps and I *won't* be a Holding Shell who forgets the face of her child."

"So you believe me now."

"Maybe I always did."

"You don't know that your baby will end up in the Heaps."

"It doesn't matter," Freesia said, hugging herself. "There's something wrong with this place. I knew it the first day when I saw the blood, but I let myself be fooled by all this!" She flung her arms around to include the impressive surroundings. "I'm going home to my family. Help me. Come with me."

"No!" Devora said. Freesia didn't understand. She might have a home, but Devora didn't. Here in the White Palace she had finally found a place of refuge—shelter and food with an element of safety, despite last night's terrifying dream.

The Matron's high-pitched tone broke in on their conversation. "So this is where you've been hiding! Freesia, it's late and you need your rest. Return to your room at once!"

"Just a minute," Freesia said, her neck breaking out in red splotches.

"And you!" the Matron harped, glaring at Devora. "You're always in the midst of trouble, aren't you?"

Devora lowered her eyes and without thinking rested her hands on her uniform, smoothing the cloth and accidentally exposing her growing belly. "I'm sorry," she said meekly.

The Matron's sharp eyes widened, taking in the shape of Devora's rounded stomach. "Why, you filthy girl!" she shouted and then lowered her voice. "Go to your room immediately.

First thing tomorrow morning, I'm having you exiled. The likes of you isn't even worth the cost or effort of an Extraction."

"But ..."

"Go pack your bag. Your time here is over."

Fury raged in Devora's chest. She longed to scratch out the Matron's eyes. Or maybe Freesia's. Would there ever be a time when she could choose her own destiny? Would she ever have more value than a piece of trash? She stumbled back to her room, choking back her angry sobs. If it hadn't been for Freesia's disappearance, she'd have escaped the Matron's notice a while longer—at least until Solange could help her.

After pacing in her room for a few moments, Devora heard a knock. "It's Freesia. Open the door. Please!"

"Go away!"

Freesia tapped again. "Let me in," she begged. "I think the Matron's coming."

"You've already made my life miserable. Why can't you just leave me alone?" Devora whispered as she tugged Freesia inside and fastened the lock on the door.

"Look, Devora, the Matron would have noticed your stomach any day now. You couldn't have gone on hiding it for much longer."

"Yes I could!" Devora insisted. After all, Freesia didn't know about Solange.

A key rattled in the lock and panic flickered across Freesia's face.

"In there!" Devora hissed, shoving Freesia into the closet. "And wait until I tell you it's safe to come back out."

The Matron stomped into the room, dumping a canvas bag on the neatly made bed. "Put your personal effects in here. You're leaving first thing in the morning. Program failures don't get second chances!"

Devora trembled, hearing Solange's words echoed by the Matron. *Program failures don't get second chances.* Her heart pounded as she also remembered Solange's warning that if her pregnancy was discovered she would be banished to the wilderness to fend for herself.

The Matron hurried away and Devora felt a tap on her shoulder as she locked her door. "What?" she said, whirling around, expecting to see that Freesia had barged out of the closet without awaiting her signal.

Solange smiled at her. "You look troubled, child. Tell me about it."

"The Matron knows I'm pregnant." She desperately hoped Freesia would stay hidden.

"Of course she does. I knew that."

Devora stared at Solange. Was it her imagination or had the glow around her faded? "I forgot. You're always with me." It was true. She had forgotten that there was no need for Freesia to continue hiding—Solange would already know of the other girl's presence.

"Yes, I am. And I've been so happy to see that you've not been talking to that silly girl."

Devora's eyes darted toward the closet door again. "Do you mean Freesia?" she asked, surprised.

"Of course, child."

Her heart beating faster, Devora said, "No ... no, I haven't been talking to her at all." *How was it possible that Solange did not know?*

"Wonderful! Now, I may not appear for several days, but don't worry, I'm always—"

"—with me," Devora muttered, adding, "Please, before you go, tell me what to do. I was thinking I should run away and find somewhere safe to hide."

Frowning, Solange said, "Absolutely not! You must go where the Matron sends you. It's necessary for my plan—" She stopped.

"Plan? You have a plan for me?" Devora grasped at the word like it was a sacred drop of water in the sweltering noonday sun.

"Yes, I do, Devora, and you mustn't try to escape. If you do, Lord Drake will send his Enforcers to track you down and their dogs will tear you apart."

Devora shuddered, looking deep into Solange's eyes as she searched for the affection she once thought was there. She saw nothing.

Solange faded away again and Devora grabbed the canvas bag. "You can come out now," she said, shuffling across the room and tapping on the closet door.

"What did the Matron want? All I could hear was muffled voices."

"She gave me this bag so I could pack. She said she's sending me away in the morning."

"I'm so sorry I got you into trouble," Freesia said, crumpling onto Devora's bed.

You should be, Devora thought, opening her bureau drawer. Aloud, she asked, "What did the Matron mean earlier by an 'Extraction'?"

Eyes wide, Freesia said, "No, you can't think of doing that! It's when they end your … pregnancy."

Devora spun around. "You mean they could get rid of this?" she said bitterly. "Well, they could, but according to the Matron, I'm not worth the cost or effort." She shivered at the thought of being dumped somewhere tomorrow. Alone. Not even having the lying Solange or nagging Freesia nearby. "Can I get one of these Extractions someplace else?"

"I … I don't know," Freesia said. "I didn't even know about the procedure until Kat first mentioned it. Then I heard some of the other girls talking. Maybe my doctor at home ... oh, this is all my fault. I'm really sorry that the Matron is sending you away."

"Don't bother about it. She can't send me away tomorrow."

"What? Why?"

"Because I'm going away with you tonight." Devora grabbed the bag and stuffed in the meagre belongings that had been allotted to her since becoming a ward girl. The Matron might have learned that she was pregnant, but Devora had learned something equally important—Solange didn't know about Freesia being in her room. Therefore, Solange was *not* always with her. Nor did Devora think Solange cared what happened to her future.

Besides, Freesia had a home to go to, a place where she belonged, and Freesia *needed* Devora's help to escape the White Palace. *And* Freesia knew a doctor. For once, Devora was choosing her own path.

"I've heard that Lord Drake will send something called Enforcers with hunting dogs to track us," Devora whispered, unable to keep the terrifying thought to herself.

"Where did you hear that?"

She shrugged. She wasn't ready to talk about Solange. Not yet.

Freesia said, "It doesn't matter. It's probably a rumour, but just in case, we'll be careful."

They stayed huddled in Devora's room until well after midnight, working out a plan of escape. When all was quiet, they slipped into the hallway and made their way through darkened corridors and shadowy staircases to the depths of the building.

Crouching behind a tower of crates piled high with bananas and pineapples, the two of them waited until just before dawn when a delivery truck pulled up to the loading dock next to the kitchen.

When the driver had unloaded the last crate, he radioed the security gate. "I'm going to grab a coffee in the kitchen and then I'm out of here."

"It's now or never," Freesia whispered, creeping toward the back of the truck after he'd gone inside.

The stench hung in the air like a thick blanket, making Devora grab her stomach and gag. "It's like the Heaps," she whispered as she climbed inside.

Freesia, who was plugging her nose, hissed, "Try it. Like this!"

Devora pinched her nostrils together and gulped air in through her mouth. "Better," she agreed, nodding.

The girls pressed forward, guided by the eerie light cast from the single bare bulb at the loading dock. They picked their way into the truck, stepping over browned cabbage leaves and empty crates.

"There's nothing to hide behind," Devora said, her voice strained with fear.

"Just go as far back as you can and lie flat."

She followed Freesia but continued to dart glances back over her shoulder.

"Hurry!"

Squatting down to the floor, Devora touched something soft and withdrew her hand in surprise. "Oh," she muttered.

"What is it?" Freesia asked, her voice nasal as she continued to pinch her nose.

Devora stretched her hand out again and felt around. "A blanket," she answered, sighing and moistening her dry lips.

The girls dropped to the floor and tucked themselves under the blanket, lying as flat as they could. Devora cursed the growing bump in her stomach and shifted her body sideways. She hated the merciless reminder of Jaron and his betrayal. He was worse than a rat—at least a rat never pretended to have anything but its own self-interest in mind. But Jaron ...

Her thoughts were interrupted by the driver's return. He slammed the back doors, plunging them into darkness.

Listening to Freesia's muted breathing, Devora's confidence in the girl wavered. After all, Jaron had used her, Benjamin had abandoned her, and Solange had lied to her. Why should she trust anyone else?

"Are you okay?" Freesa asked as the truck rumbled.

"I think so." Devora rubbed her side. The truck had jostled her so hard she'd bounced up and landed awkwardly on her hip.

This time she was prepared for the first sign of betrayal. She balled her hands into tight fists, determined to sacrifice Freesia or anyone else in order to save her own skin.

15

The High Priestess

Jaron ran his finger along the blade of the knife. In a sickening way it was his one tie to humanity—Ansel. He longed for space, a place of freedom. A place to call home. He pounded his fists into his cot.

"You're finally acting like you belong here," Benjamin said from the opposite side of the room. They were the only two Cadets housed here, surrounded by empty beds. There hadn't been many passes from the Heaps lately.

"Like you said, I'm training to be an Enforcer. It's time I behaved like one."

"Sure," Benjamin said, turning away, his voice unusually subdued. "I knew you'd come around."

Was it his imagination, or did his former friend sound disappointed?

Benjamin finished straightening his uniform and polishing his boots. "Now I get to meet *him* too."

Staring at his own distorted refection in the blade, Jaron observed the colour draining from his cheeks. "Who?"

"Lord Drake. I'm going to his castle tonight for my graduation. You're coming too."

"No, I'm not," Jaron said, squeezing the knife.

"Yes, you are. I requested it."

The steel of the blade bit into Jaron's clenched fingers. He barely noticed. "Why did you do that?"

"At first I wanted to show off that I graduated and you didn't. But now that the word is out about your fight, I figure Lord Drake will give me a better assignment if he sees you there beside me."

"I wouldn't count on it," Jaron mumbled as Benjamin left the room.

The news of Jaron's victory had spread like a fever since he'd returned to the barracks three days ago. On the night of the fight, Jaron had broken away from the "celebration" and bolted for the showers, turning the hot water on full blast. The steam attacked his skin and he welcomed the searing heat, begging it to cleanse his thoughts as well. It hadn't worked. And now, days later, he still carried the images like glossy photographs: Ansel's lifeless body and Lord Drake's face alive with rage.

He pulled a clean uniform from his locker. Leaning forward to tie his boots, he heard a crackle in his shirt pocket. Surprised, he retrieved a single sheet of paper. Unfolding it, he held his breath as he read:

> Jaron,
>
> The Ancient Way has demanded my life for yours. Your mother would grieve to learn that you know nothing about your family's heritage as Keepers of the Key. She did her best, hiding you from the enemy by smuggling you into the Heaps. She could think of nothing better. Forgive her.
>
> Time is short for you. Now that the enemy has found you, he will try to deceive you and steal what is rightfully yours. Guard yourself. Don't commit violence out of revenge, for that will cost you your inheritance.
>
> Your Servant,
> Ansel

How could Ansel say so much and yet so little? Jaron reread the message, searching for more. All he found were unanswered questions.

He closed his eyes, trying to remember his mother's face. He succeeded for a split second as her image appeared like an apparition. His heart skipped a beat as he saw that she wasn't alone. This time, a man with laughing eyes and a giggling girl with a mass of blond curls joined his mother. *Who are they?* he wondered, but the random window on his past slammed shut.

Why had his mother hidden him in the Heaps?

The key hung like a lead weight around his neck. He debated hiding it, but where?

"A Keeper of the Key," he whispered, recalling Lord Drake's ferocity when he couldn't snatch the key from Jaron. Somehow, Jaron gained protection by wearing this little bit of metal. And somehow this little bit of metal also gained protection from him. He determined to keep it with him—always.

"Time for our injections," Benjamin announced, stomping back into the room.

Jaron slipped Ansel's note under his mattress and followed Benjamin to the doctor's office. The injections sedated the Enforcers, counteracting the effects of the pills in order to make them appear almost civilized for a time. Jaron had only received two during his time at the barracks, on occasions when officials were touring Lord Drake's "wonderfully humane" training facility.

The doctor jabbed the needle into his arm and Jaron squeezed his eyes shut, trying to keep his wits about him. Because he didn't take the pills, the injections made him feel groggy for hours. He wished he could have avoided the doctor this evening, knowing that tonight, of all nights, he needed to be alert as he entered the house of his enemy.

"Lower it!" Captain Mar ordered.

The gatekeeper obeyed and the spine-chilling reverberation of metal scraping stone echoed in the night. The weathered wooden planks on the surface of the drawbridge seemed an inappropriate backdrop for the bulletproof glass encasing the guards' station.

The others trampled across as if it were nothing. Jaron forced himself to move forward, but he couldn't focus his eyes ahead. It was stupid, he knew, but he stared dazedly down over the side of the bridge as if looking for something.

A blinding streak of light bolted from the darkest depths of the abyss below and soared up through the night sky. "Did you see that?" Jaron asked, rubbing his hand over his eyes and blinking.

"See what, the Chasm?" the trainer said, stopping to peer down into the blackened depths. "It's just a 300-foot trench across and down," he said. "If the fall doesn't kill you, the rattlesnakes waiting at the bottom will."

"No! The light. It swooped up from the bottom and shot into the sky," Jaron insisted, swaying. He resisted the compulsion to lie down to combat the dizziness induced by his injection.

"Right," the trainer said, prodding Jaron along in an attempt to catch up with the others. "Next you'll be saying you see the lions loose in the streets."

"What?"

"The lions. At Lord Drake's hunting grounds."

"He hunts lions?"

"No," the trainer laughed. "The lions hunt … prey. Human prey."

"Oh," Jaron replied, realizing his world was expanding exponentially beyond the Heaps. What if the ten year-spans he'd spent at the rotten core of the Realm of Leviathon turned out to be the kindest part of his existence?

When they reached the end of the drawbridge, they paused in front of two metal-clad doors that swung open before them on silent hinges. Jaron exhaled and his breath escaped into the chilled air, making him desperate to slip away just as quietly.

Benjamin was the first to strut through the entrance and into the castle's great hall. Jaron stayed near the back of the group as the doors clamped shut behind them. Now there could be no doubt that the stories in the discarded newspapers were true—the opulent party they were walking into was no fairytale.

Hundreds of people had already gathered and Jaron wondered how many times the drawbridge had slithered across the chasm only to be whisked away, leaving Lord Drake and his guests protected by the invisible shield of snakes.

"Do they do this for every new Enforcer?" Jaron asked, his injection wearing off enough to be aware of the *plakin* crystals dripping from the chandeliers. He'd seen pictures of the semi-precious stones in his scavenged newspapers, but the two-dimensional matte photographs did not do justice to the brilliant rainbow prisms that now glittered overhead.

"Only the ones who successfully kill their first time out," the trainer replied. "Move forward," he added, prodding Jaron down the throng of men and women.

Jaron pressed through the crowd side-by-side with Benjamin. The male guests were wearing starched shirts and black jackets with matching trousers. The women's attire was like nothing he'd ever seen—wispy garments billowing like multi-coloured clouds.

The guests parted and Jaron gasped as he caught sight of *her*. Her golden curls cascaded down over her shoulders and spilled onto her silken garment.

"Joelle!" he whispered, as the image of the giggling Five-Year once again involuntarily burst into his thoughts before melting away like wax.

"Welcome," she said, her smile capturing the breath from his lungs. She seemed to have absorbed all of the light from the room.

Instinctively, he bowed before her and Benjamin scurried to do the same.

A trumpet sounded and Lord Drake paraded into the room and placed his arm possessively around the shoulders of the radiant woman.

Jaron thought he observed her recoil slightly at Lord Drake's touch. Then her eyes sought out Jaron's and he felt as if she gazed through him, into his thoughts, his soul.

"Welcome," she said again, and this time it seemed she was speaking only to him.

Scrambling for something fitting to say, Jaron remembered the words from Ansel's letter. "I am your servant," he replied, bowing again.

The orchestra began to play and Jaron stepped back as Lord Drake led her onto the dance floor. With every turn she searched for Jaron, her eyes locked in silent appeal . . . but for what?

"Everyone stares at her the first time they see her," his trainer said, poking Jaron in the ribs.

"Is she ... *his?*"

The trainer laughed. "They might teach you how to read in the Heaps, but they don't teach you much about women, do they?"

Jaron's face grew warm. "Who is she?" he asked, captivated as she whirled around the room.

"*She* is the High Priestess of Leviathon," the trainer answered, as if that explained everything.

The song ended and the audience clapped and whistled. Lord Drake led his partner over to Jaron and Benjamin. "My dear," Lord Drake said, his eyes like daggers, "allow me to present to you our two esteemed Cadets, Jaron and Benjamin."

The High Priestess nodded her acknowledgement and extended her hand, touching Jaron's arm. "I am honoured to meet you."

Jaron's heart lurched and his arm felt like it had been brushed with fire. He feared that once she withdrew her hand, a piece of him would go with it. "It is I who am honoured to meet you, High ... High Priestess," he stuttered with the unfamiliar words.

The music resumed and Jaron soaked in her image as she danced away in the arms of his enemy.

Suddenly, Captain Mar rushed across the room, his boots scuffing on the alabaster tiles. He tapped Lord Drake on the shoulder and the Supreme Ruler bowed to the High Priestess before turning an intense scowl on the interloper.

Jaron was too far away to hear their conversation, but he watched as Lord Drake motioned to the band to stop playing.

"Ladies and gentlemen, please forgive me. I have an urgent matter to attend to," Lord Drake announced. "May I have the members of the Enforcer squad meet me in the drawing room?"

The trainer shoved Jaron toward the Enforcers that followed Lord Drake. The High Priestess drifted amongst the men dressed in khaki uniforms. *A rose among thorns*, Jaron thought.

Once in the drawing room, Captain Mar gave the orders to the squad. "Dangerous criminals have escaped," he said. "Two mental patients from the maximum security detention centre have disappeared."

Benjamin stood tensely beside Jaron, grinning as Captain Mar gave the order to kill. Enforcers didn't take prisoners.

Feeling an unseen tug, as if someone had a string tied to his head and was guiding his movements, Jaron turned to find the High Priestess gazing at him.

Captain Mar's voice faded into the background. The High Priestess nodded at Jaron and he returned the sentiment, startled at her attention. The noise of cheering Enforcers broke into Jaron's thoughts and he tore his eyes away from her.

"You understand what you have to do?" his trainer asked.

Jaron blinked. He had no idea what the trainer was talking about. "I think I missed a little," he admitted.

The trainer's lips set in a firm line. "Distracted, were you?" he asked, not waiting for an answer. "I'll give you the short version. Tonight is your test. You get to come with us on this mission."

"You mean to catch the criminals?" Jaron felt as though he'd been struck.

Nodding, the trainer stepped aside as Lord Drake approached.

"Congratulations, Jaron," Lord Drake said, baring his teeth. "Tonight you get to do what all Cadets dream of once they've completed their training."

The Leader of the Realm marched away, leaving Jaron to digest the meaning of his words.

"What did he mean?" Jaron was finally able to ask his trainer as they were swept up in the tide of green leaving the drawing room.

"Tonight is the night for your ultimate revenge. You'll get to perform the Eradication."

"Who—" Jaron began, unable to complete his thought.

"Who else, but your Holding Shell, your mother. Her name is Freesia."

"To the barracks!" Captain Mar shouted as they exited the ballroom and marched once again along the timbers of the drawbridge. "It's time to release the hounds!"

Jaron's breathing now came in shallow gasps. He slipped to the rear of the group and paused in the middle of the bridge, surrounded by impossibilities. Behind him was the threatening presence of Lord Drake, on either side of him was certain death in the trench crawling with rattlesnakes, and ahead of him lay the road to revenge—the one he desperately longed to escape.

"You're still here?"

Fire flamed in Jaron's face as he turned to face the High Priestess. "I stopped … lost in thought, I suppose."

Her hand brushed Jaron's cheek and he reminded himself to keep breathing. Then her fingers dropped to his neck and traced the cord that held his key. "Tell me about this."

He slipped the string over his head and held it out for her to see. "It's just a key. I'm not even sure what it unlocks," he said, wishing he could whisk it back and hide it from her. His treasured possession dimmed in her presence.

Her eyes stayed fixed on the key. "I think it's a symbol of family," she whispered. "Given to you by your mother, right?"

How did she guess? "Yes," he answered.

"Soon you'll give it away for love," she said, lifting her eyes from the key.

"Yes, High Priestess," he said, believing her. It all made sense now.

She smiled. "You mustn't be so formal, Jaron. It would please me if you would simply call me by my name."

Joelle, he thought as the unfamiliar name blazed into his consciousness again and inhabited him as if it belonged.

"Solange," she said, taking his hand.

"Solange?" he repeated, confusion shaking his concentration. He tripped and the key flew from his hand, landing only a few finger-spans from the edge of the drawbridge.

Leaping forward, he clawed at the frayed string. He wouldn't lose the key now! He finally knew what the key unlocked. Home wasn't a place with a roof and door; it was a feeling—"love," as Solange had called it. Belonging to some*one* rather than some*thing*.

"Go pass your test, Jaron, and we will meet again."

16
Walking the Gauntlet

"Are you sure you know the way?"

Freesia gritted her teeth. Devora had asked the same question at least ten times in the last hour. "My parents' farm is north," she said again. "So we'll follow the Gauntlet River until we reach the Northern Canal."

"When will we reach the river?" Devora asked, hoisting the sack up higher on her back.

Freesia stopped. "I don't know, Devora!" she snapped. "Stop asking me over and over again. It's not every day that I become a fugitive who rides in the back of a cabbage truck!" She instantly regretted her sharp words when she saw Devora's shoulders slump. "Let's stop for a rest," she suggested as a peace offering.

They found a shady spot underneath an evergreen tree thick with fragrant needles, and Freesia rummaged through the small sack she carried and retrieved a jar of water. "Have a sip," she offered.

Devora reached for the jar, and then pulled her hand back.

"We've been walking all morning," Freesia pointed out. "Aren't you thirsty?"

Nodding, Devora clamped her hands around the jar. "Thank you," she whispered, gulping two mouthfuls. "No one's ever shared water with me before."

Freesia stared at the peculiar girl who had lived through so much and yet still seemed to know nothing about life. "Didn't you share with your friends, Benjamin and Jaron?"

"Bits of food, but never water. Not even Jaron shared his water."

"Jaron was the kindest of the two, then?"

The muscles around Devora's mouth twitched as she sat stiffly, breaking dried pine needles one by one from a little pile she'd amassed beside her. "I used to think so," she said, lowering her gaze.

"You must miss him terribly."

Devora raised her head, a lone tear trailing down her cheek. "I hate him," she hissed, clutching her stomach. "He did this to me!"

Recalling her own experience, Freesia said, "Why are you so angry? When Dr. Lyson performed my procedure it wasn't pleasant, but I really didn't mind it too much."

"What did Dr. Lyson do to you?" Devora asked, her voice tense.

Freesia explained the procedure: the medication, the needles, and the test tubes.

"That's it! That's all that happened to you!" Devora collapsed on the ground, shaking in bitter laughter until tears soaked her face and her shoulders quaked in anguished sobs.

When Devora finally quieted enough to tell Freesia how she'd become pregnant, the fear and shame covered her like a veil. Obviously the betrayal of a beloved friend had shattered her.

Freesia's horror spilled out in response. "He's vile! No wonder you hate him! How could you even stand to see him day after day in the Heaps?"

Devora blinked hard. "I guess I didn't know it was him then," she said. "The night was dark, black as coal."

"Then how do you know it was him that hurt you?"

"I remembered later," Devora said and then clamped her lips tightly together.

Freesia didn't ask any more as the two of them gathered their belongings and set out through the forest. Devora trudged silently for the rest of the afternoon, and oddly enough, Freesia missed the other girl's repetitive questions and nervous chatter. It seemed that Devora had lost her drive for survival and Freesia feared that she, herself, would now have to muster up enough courage for them both.

Near sunset, Freesia instinctively headed toward the rushing sound of the Gauntlet, but it wasn't until the white water rapids sprang into view that she breathed a sigh of relief. "We've made it," she cried, skipping toward the riverbank.

Devora, pale with drooping shoulders, bent to scoop up a handful of the ice-cold water and splash it on her face. "Can we sleep here?" she pleaded, her voice hoarse.

In school, Freesia had studied until she'd surpassed her classmates. Reading, writing, and mathematics were all lessons in which she had excelled. She'd been driven to achieve the coveted honour of being chosen for the Maternity Program, for no other vocation brought such pride to a parent or such admiration from others. But in this moment, Freesia overlooked all of her celebrated education and remembered a simple lesson learned while hunting with her father: when the prey crossed a river, their hound, Challis, lost the scent.

"We can't stay here. We have to cross so that the dogs will lose our trail. Take off your shoes."

Freesia waited for Devora's response, sure that the girl would argue. Instead, she obediently unlaced her brown rubber-soled shoes while Freesia slipped out of her low-heeled slippers.

"I'll go first," Freesia volunteered, stepping into the water. "You know how to swim, right?" The initial shock of cold to her toes instantly gave way to a dull ache as numbness set in.

From behind her, Devora called out, "What?"

Freesia stopped and spun around, almost losing her balance. "If it's over our heads, we'll have to swim through the water."

"Over … over our h-heads? No! I can't!"

Taking a deep breath, Freesia lifted her dress and waded deeper into the churning water. It climbed to her knees, her hips, her waist—it was no use! She was not even a quarter of the way across and the water swirling in front of her grew midnight black. She sloshed back to the side. "We have to cross at a place where the river is more shallow."

"What if we can't?"

"We will. We have to. If we don't and they come looking for us, the dogs will find us."

"I should never have come with you," Devora shuddered.

Freesia pulled out a new gown from her pack, still shivering even after she'd changed into something dry. "Stay here, then," she said, her body trembling.

"I—"

"Those are your two choices. Stay, or come with me." She spun around and headed downstream.

"Wait!" Devora cried. "Where are you going? I thought we needed to go in the other direction."

"We do. But if they follow our trail this way, they'll think we're going south. Hopefully it'll take them longer to find our scent once we cross to the other side."

Guided by the moonlight, the girls journeyed south. Freesia had lost nearly all hope of finding a crossing when, around a bend, the river widened. Grasping one another's hands, they splashed through the water, slipping on rounded stones as they made their way across.

Once they reached the other side, Devora begged for relief from the painfully cold water but Freesia gripped her hand tightly, dragging her north through ankle-deep water for at least half an hour before agreeing to emerge onto dry land.

The girls rubbed their feet, trying to coax the feeling back into their toes as their teeth chattered.

"I'll never be warm again," Devora complained, pulling a rough woollen nightgown from her sack and wrapping it around her legs.

Freesia imagined a roaring fire in the stone fireplace in her family's farmhouse. It wouldn't be too much farther. She hoped they would reach home by tomorrow evening. What would her parents say when she turned up, unannounced, a fugitive from the maternity program? "Do you think you can walk a little more? We should find somewhere safe to spend the night," she said.

Devora uncovered her feet and pushed them awkwardly into her stiff work shoes. She stood up. "I'm ready."

They scrambled to a hill covered by a thicket of trees. "This will do," Freesia said, wishing they dared light a fire for warmth and protection. It was a wasted wish. Even if the fire wouldn't proclaim their position to any pursuers, the simple fact remained that they had no matches.

The night noises dimmed as even the river seemed more hushed under the dark sky. Freesia drifted off to sleep and dreamed of almond cookies and warm cocoa.

Near dawn she awoke to Devora's terrified gasp, "Oh no!"

"What's wrong?" Freesia asked, rolling to her side. Then she heard it. Above the whirling splash of the river rapids the sound pierced the air. The two girls hastily shoved the extra clothing they'd used as blankets into their sacks and stumbled further into the forest, motivated by the distant din of barking dogs.

17
Into the Fire

The image of the High Priestess burned in Jaron's brain, and it seemed as if everything else had faded like mist. She had promised to see him again, but first he must pass this test. Then he'd be welcomed back into the castle of Lord Drake— where she'd be waiting.

Solange, shimmering in her spotless gown, could not have understood what was required to pass this test. Surely her hands had never touched death, caused death. Not like Lord Drake, whose eyes oozed cruelty. Jaron shuddered, picturing Solange trapped in Lord Drake's arms. She couldn't know! Or could she? Perhaps that's why she'd stared at Jaron, her eyes begging for freedom.

"This is different than the night I did my first kill," Benjamin whispered, perched next to Jaron on a narrow bench in the back of a truck.

"How?" Jaron asked.

"I went with four others to a hunting reserve and she was just ... there, hiding in the trees. An hour later we were on our way back to the barracks."

Jaron turned away and Benjamin tugged his arm.

"Don't act like you're better than me," he growled. "We both grew up scavenging in the same place, dumped there by our no-good mothers!" He grabbed a handful of pills and choked them back with water from a battered canteen. "Turns out *your* mother is *really* crazy, though. That's why we're searching all over the countryside trying to find her and her loony friend."

Jaron whipped his head back, glaring. "Whatever my mother is, she's better than you ... and me."

"That's your biggest flaw, Jaron. You still feel remorse." Benjamin grinned, his stained teeth pale in the moonlight. "Funny thing, though, your oversized guilt didn't seem to bother you the night you stole my shelter."

Jaron shook his head in disbelief. How could Benjamin not understand? "You hurt her, Benjamin," he said, remembering the blood-encrusted cut along Devora's lip.

"Why should I care?" Benjamin asked. "My mother, my Holding Shell, threw me away."

Knowing his former ally had misunderstood, Jaron watched as the window of Benjamin's lucidity slipped away. It was too late to correct the mistakes of the past.

The truck braked and the Enforcers spilled out the back, pushing Jaron along with them. Captain Mar gave his orders. "Find them, but don't kill them. Bring them back here so Jaron can do the Eradication."

The Enforcers fanned out to conduct their search. The hounds dropped their snouts, routing for the scent of the escaped women.

Jaron wandered through the darkness, guided only by the narrow beam cast from his battery-operated torch. As the noises of the others faded behind him, he imagined himself in another place and time, dancing. Each time his partner twirled around, her face would change—Solange, then Devora, then his mother.

Their search lasted through the night as one dog picked up the scent, then another. Beams of light bounced through the trees as Enforcers raced to be part of the latest "discovery."

Jaron kept to the edge of the group, following them but not a part of them. At dawn all of the Enforcers gathered at the bank of the rushing river. Jaron stared at the unfamiliar sight—an abundance of fresh water. He fought the urge to jump in and be swept away.

Captain Mar conferred with his more experienced trackers. "They've crossed the river," he announced. "Return to the trucks! She's heading home."

Home? His mother was heading home?

They travelled for another hour over pitted dirt roads before the truck again screeched to a halt.

Sucking in his breath at the view, Jaron jumped from the vehicle. The crisp white farmhouse at the end of the lane eerily resembled the home he'd longed for during his year-spans in the Heaps. He'd left that faded newspaper photo behind the night he'd been hauled away, but the memory now resurfaced and his heart quickened.

The roar of the trucks must have alerted the inhabitants, because a smiling woman appeared on the porch, wiping her hands on an apron as a whistling man in overalls rounded the side of the house.

"Where is she?" Captain Mar said, meeting the woman's gentle smile with a frozen glare.

Obviously puzzled, the woman shook her head. "I don't know who you mean. It's just Layden and I who live here."

"Your daughter!" Captain Mar said, taking an abrupt step forward.

The man—Layden, Jaron presumed—moved protectively toward the woman. "Our daughter is in the Maternity Program," he said with pride. "Her first child will be a scientist."

Jaron stared at them both, wondering what connection they had to his mother. How could *their* daughter be *his* mother?

"You can wipe that smile off your face," Captain Mar said, lifting his hand to point an accusing finger at them. "Your daughter has abandoned her duty and escaped."

"That's impossible!" the woman said. "Freesia wouldn't do that! She worked so hard to get into that program."

Maternity Program? Jaron thought. What were they talking about? They were chasing his mother who had escaped from the insane ward, weren't they? His disappointment confused him. He didn't want to kill his mother, but he realized how much he'd longed for the opportunity to catch even one glimpse of her.

"Tie them up and search the house!" Captain Mar ordered.

Two Enforcers ran forward with thick cords of black rope and shoved Layden and his wife to the ground as four others pounded up the stairs and smashed through the door.

The sound of breaking glass echoed from inside the home's peaceful exterior and he hated to know it was being violated. Jaron bit back angry tears.

Benjamin was the first to emerge from the house. "It's empty," he said to Captain Mar.

"Check the barn!" the captain roared.

Sputtering dirt, Layden pleaded, "Believe us, she's not here. We would tell you."

Captain Mar grinned. "I believe you actually would tell us. But just in case I'm wrong—" he stopped, motioning to Jaron, saying, "Get the jug of fuel from the back of the truck."

With his heart hammering, Jaron raced to obey. What was going on? These people had done nothing and now their home was being ripped apart. The pungent odour of fuel stung his nose as he carried the heavy jug back to Captain Mar, who was now leisurely lighting a fresh cigar.

"Today's your impromptu lesson in arson," Captain Mar said after a deep inhale and an expert puff. "Go inside and spray the petrol around."

"Wh-What?"

"Dump the fuel, Cadet," he ordered, drawing his gun. "Now, or I'll shoot you in the head."

The jug slapped against Jaron's leg, splashing liquid as his head throbbed from the offensive smell. He climbed the stairs and entered the home—a real home. Rugs scattered the floor and cushioned chairs filled the room. He tipped the jug forward and closed his eyes, wishing he could also shut off the senses of his ears and nose. The stench of the fuel would ruin this place. It would kill the fragile aroma of spices now barely discernable.

While splattering fuel onto the kitchen floor, Jaron bumped into the table and glanced up to see a half-filled mug of tea. He reached to feel the outside of the cup—it was still warm.

Then he froze. Beside the cup lay a red book with the title, *The Ancient Way*. The outline of a key was stamped on the cover. "Ansel," he whispered.

Not willing to see the book destroyed, Jaron tucked it into the pocket of his trousers, hoping this one saving gesture could somehow atone for his act of desecration.

Tears flooded his face and mixed with his sweat as he sloshed the liquid around, dousing photographs and furniture. When the jug was finally empty, he wiped his face with his sleeve and forced himself to walk back outside, but he kept his eyes away from Layden, who was still facedown in the dirt.

"Stand them up," Captain Mar ordered.

Jaron assisted the woman to her feet. Tears trailed down her dust-covered face. "I don't understand," she whispered.

Layden stood, his face only finger-spans from Jaron's.

"I'm sorry," Jaron mouthed.

"I understand," Layden said softly, patting Jaron on the chest. "They forced you to do it. It's only a house filled with things. It's the people that make it home."

Jaron pulled the book from his pocket, wanting to slip it to Layden unnoticed.

The man's eyes widened. "Keep it hidden," he cautioned. "I never understood most of it, but I know it's important. A man once gave his life to protect it . . . and her." Layden grabbed Jaron's hand, pleading, "Find our girl! Keep her safe."

"Move, Cadet!" Captain Mar said, waving his gun.

Jaron turned away to tuck the book out of sight just as the rapid pop of bullets echoed like thunder. His knees buckled.

A snarling shepherd dog charged from the barn. Another lone shot rang out and the animal collapsed.

"Now you can torch the house," Captain Mar ordered, tossing the box of matches at him.

"You want me to burn it?" Jaron asked, staggering at his first glimpse of the two lifeless bodies. Layden and his wife had been executed, and now their house would be destroyed. Wherever their daughter was, she no longer had a home—or a family.

Jaron wanted to scream. Run. Hit something.

"Hurry up or I'll kill you too," Captain Mar ordered, levelling his gun at Jaron's forehead.

Dragging one foot in front of the other, Jaron focused on the red door of the house as he gripped the box of matches in one hand and wrenched at the string holding his key with the other. The rotting twine broke free and he clutched the key. He was a coward, not worthy to wear anything that reminded him of his mother, or Ansel.

He struck the match and lowered the fragile flame into the puddle of fuel on the steps of the porch. The fire burst like a gunshot into the house and he stood there, captivated, as his key slipped from his hand and thudded into the dirt. He shook himself free of his stupor, reaching down for the key just as a ravenous flame leapt back, lunging at his outstretched arm.

His flesh sizzled and a black cloud roared forth from the house, filling his lungs until a quiet darkness cocooned him.

18
Caught

"I have to stop," Devora begged, wheezing as she tried to catch her breath. For years she'd shaded herself from the afternoon sun in the Heaps, conserving her energy and waiting until the day cooled before scavenging for water. Never having had much strength, she was now even further impeded by her condition.

Freesia frowned. "We'll be caught. We have to keep going."

Envying Freesia's endurance, Devora said, "We haven't heard the dogs again. We outsmarted them."

"Maybe. We'll stop for just a few minutes. I'm dying to see my parents."

Freesia spoke with a longing Devora couldn't understand. There was no one she wanted to see, to depend on. From now on Devora would be the only one to look out for Devora. "One for one," she muttered, reciting the familiar phrase, and for the first time she really meant it.

"What does *that* mean?" asked Freesia.

"It was the only thing we were allowed to say to each other in the Heaps. It means you survive by looking out for number one—yourself."

"That's awful! I can't imagine not having my parents or friends to talk to."

"It's no big deal," Devora said, wishing Freesia would stop sounding so sympathetic. *No guilt*, she reminded herself, kicking at the pebbles in the dirt. Hearing an animal howling in the distance sent cold chills down her legs. "I'm ready now," she gulped, struggling to her feet.

"Don't worry," Freesia soothed. "It's only a coyote and it's a long ways away."

They pressed on through the hayfield. Freesia's promise of cool spring water along with a mound of warm gingerbread once they reached the farm gave Devora the incentive to keep moving.

"Do your parents have other children?" Devora asked, wondering how many mouths would be fighting for the same morsel of gingerbread.

"No," Freesia said. "But I remember having a brother, Aaron. He died a long time ago."

"What happened to him?"

"I don't know. Mama and Papa would never speak of him. They said it was better that way."

"Oh," Devora said, her back muscles in spasms.

"We're here!" Freesia screeched suddenly, breaking into a run. "It's just over this hill!"

"You go on," Devora said, mopping beads of sweat from her forehead. "I'll catch up in a minute."

Freesia disappeared from view and Devora paused as a welcome breeze washed over her. Her rumbling stomach begged her to keep moving, but she hesitated. She had no idea what families were even like. Maybe Freesia's parents wouldn't want an extra person around. Maybe she should just disappear now and search for a doctor on her own.

The coyote howled again and her eyes darted around the field, searching for the unseen predator. Running away wouldn't be as easy as she'd hoped. The serene-looking countryside held an element of horror, much like the Heaps. Worries of rats and traitorous friends had now traded places with coyotes and rattlesnakes.

An instant later, the air filled with an even more piercing sound than the coyote's cry. Freesia's terror-filled wail resonated as she screamed from somewhere beyond the hill. "Help! Help!"

Devora's body stiffened. Her first instinct was to find a place to hide. A few arm-spans away stood a single tree, its lower branches within reach. Soaked in sweat, she heaved herself up, panting, crawling only as far as the second branch. She didn't even try to pretend to herself that she was high enough to be safe. The Enforcer's dogs would soon find her and rip her apart.

She waited, straining her ears, but heard nothing more. Then she saw Freesia stagger up over the crest of the hill, her robe smeared with soot and blood. "Devora, Devora, where are you?" Freesia screeched.

Shut up! Devora thought. *Whoever did this to you will hear you and find me.*

"Devora! Devora! DEVORA!"

The unrelenting call finally pulled her from the tree. It would be impossible for their pursuers not to find her with the racket Freesia was making.

Freesia tangled her arms around Devora, squeezing her.

Devora pried herself loose.

"The house ..." Freesia sputtered, her arms now sagging at her side. "House gone ... ashes and smoke."

"You're covered in blood," Devora said.

"Gone ... dead ... shot," Freesia said, sinking down in the waist-high grass.

"What are you talking about?" Devora demanded.

Freesia gazed into the distance and said nothing, her face still.

Stupid rat! What if they're chasing you? Devora thought, glaring at her. *I guess they'd be here by now*, she reasoned, answering her own silent question.

She crept forward, awkwardly hunching over to stay hidden by the grass. *Just one peek*, she promised herself.

From the top of the hill she could see the trail of smoke slithering from the charred embers of what used to be a house. Dozens of Heapdwellers could have been sheltered in a building that size and Freesia had lived there alone with her parents! Silently, she moved closer, her heart pounding with jealous rage laced with terror.

She saw the woman first. The mother—Freesia's Holding Shell. A vulture hovered beside the lifeless body ... waiting. The man lay an arm-span away, his hand stretched out toward the woman.

Devora spun around and ran up the hill, gripping her belly that jostled with every step. "Get up," she hissed, tugging Freesia's arm. "We have to get away!"

The other girl sat staring straight ahead.

"Hurry! They'll find us," Devora said.

But again Freesia didn't move. Devora wished she dared to run away by herself. If only she knew where to go.

"You have to save your baby," Devora said, positioning her face directly in front of Freesia's.

Freesia blinked and began to tremble. Devora grabbed her by the arm and yanked her to her feet. "We're going back the way we came until we reach the last stream we crossed. Then I'll think of something."

This time they set out with Devora in the lead and Freesia stumbling behind. As they cut back across the field, Devora obsessed over her aggravation at Freesia's need for her help. *I wish I could just leave you here.*

The sun had set by the time they reached the edge of the stream that bordered the field. Devora plunged into the water and dragged Freesia with her. She decided it didn't matter which direction they went, as long as they left the tracking dogs confused. Since she'd retraced their steps to the river, she hoped the Enforcers would follow the original trail to the farmhouse and then it would look like the girls had vanished. *Pretty smart thinking for a program failure*, she thought.

They'd been in the stream for no more than fifteen minutes when the sharp bark of a dog penetrated the darkness. Devora grabbed Freesia's arm and the other girl didn't flinch—it was as if she was asleep, unaware of the freezing water, the noises of the forest, or the menacing dog.

"Stop or I'll shoot!" a man ordered from the edge of the stream.

Devora positioned herself with her belly facing him. Maybe he'd shoot her in the gut and she'd still be able to live while the thing growing inside her would finally be exterminated.

"Move slowly toward me with your hands in the air," the man said.

Obeying, Devora sloshed through the water and emerged near him. It was impossible to see his face in the darkness.

"You too!" he yelled, flashing his electric torch toward Freesia. "What's wrong with her?" he asked when Freesia didn't move.

Devora wanted to march back into the water and drag Freesia out by the hair. Couldn't she see she was making the man angry? "Freesia's not herself. Do you want me to get her?"

"Freesia?" the man said, shining the torch directly onto the girl's expressionless face. Then he threw aside his gun and lunged into the water and carried her back to shore. Wrapping his jacket around her soaking feet he said, "Freesia, talk to me. It's Riak!"

Devora's mouth hung open as the stranger bent and kissed Freesia on the forehead.

"What happened to her?" he demanded.

"Who are you?" Devora whispered.

"I live at the farm next door. I've known her for years . . . we're friends."

She eyed him suspiciously. "You're more than friends," she stated.

As if to prove her right, he drew Freesia closer. "She's supposed to be in the Maternity Program," he said. "So why are the two of you stealing through the forest in the dark?"

"Why are you out here with a gun?" she hurled back. Why should she tell him anything? Maybe he was one of Lord Drake's Enforcers.

"Riak? RIAK!"

"I'm over here, Father," Riak answered.

An older man approached, his chest heaving with short breaths. "I went to see Layden," he said, staring at Freesia lying in Riak's arms.

Edging toward the river, Devora dreaded the stranger's next words. Was he the one who had massacred Freesia's parents?

"They're gone, Riak. Dead! Both of them. Bullets in their chests and their house a smoking pile of ashes."

"What?" Riak gently released Freesia and strode to Devora, grabbing her by the shoulders. "Tell me what happened," he said, gripping so hard his fingers bit into her flesh until she winced.

"Son! Let her go—she's just a child."

"She's old enough. Look at her. She's pregnant too! They're both part of that horrible program. I knew Freesia should never have gone there. They're like lab rats!"

"You can't know that, Riak," his father said, pulling his son away and speaking to Devora. "Please," he implored. "We want to help you. Tell us what happened."

Too tired to stand, she sunk down onto the muddy stones bordering the river. There was nowhere else to turn. If they had wanted to kill her, she was sure they would have done so already.

Her words trickled out slowly at first and then gushed forth as she divulged the secrets buried within the Realm of Leviathon.

"I didn't know," Riak's father groaned.

Riak caressed Freesia's cheek, but she sat immobile, unresponsive. "I'll go with them, Father."

"Of course, Son. Follow the canal to the Gauntlet River and go as far north as you can. You'll find enough berries and game for food. I'll go back ... and take care of the dead."

Devora's chest constricted as she watched Riak's gentle touch on Freesia's face. It wasn't fair! Freesia had so much!

Not even the murder of Freesia's parents could penetrate Devora's frozen heart. *So what?* she thought. Parents were unnecessary. The only thing her mother had ever taught her was that Squealing Bundles were disposable. "I want to find a doctor first."

"There's no time," Riak said. "Freesia's shock will wear off."

"Not for her—for me!" The bitter resentment choked her. Would no one *ever* put her first?

"Are you ill?"

"No ... I—"

"There's no time, unless it's an emergency." Riak put his arm around Freesia.

"Let's go," Devora said, forcing herself to stand on swollen feet as the prospect of an Extraction slipped away. She wasn't going to be the one to slow them down. Riak wouldn't care what happened to her, so she'd have to do whatever was necessary to look out for herself.

Only the strong survive.

19
Visions and Dreams

Jaron clung to a rope, his feet slicing against the jagged wall of the canyon. Think, he told himself as his raw hands started to slip. Which way to safety–up or down? Too late to decide! The rope began to stretch thin like a rubber band and he plummeted down into nothing. Speeding faster than his fear, he couldn't even hear his own cry for help. Then he ricocheted back toward the sky. Lifted by the springing rubber band, he flew higher and higher, settling on a grassy ledge covered with–snakes.

"Wake up," a golden serpent hissed before turning to devour a smaller one.

"Jaron, wake up!"

Opening his eyes, he saw only white. Where was he? He was lying down and he couldn't move. His body was paralysed.

"Have a sip."

Whoever had spoken had raised their hand in front of his mouth, offering a half-filled glass of orange juice. They also lifted his head up so that he could gulp the tart liquid that stung his parched throat.

"Wh ... eh," he mumbled, searching for words at the blurry sight of golden curls. Who was she? "Sol–"

"Tell me where it is!" she hissed.

Jaron heard a door open and a man spoke, "He needs his rest now."

"Of courssss."

Rest.

"Lullaby and goodnight."

"Mama?"

"Yes, Jaron, I'm here. Go back to sleep."

"I had a dream about a snake."

"Shh! It's okay, you'll be safe. Mama will keep you safe."

"Where's Joelle?"

"Papa took Joelle on a long trip to find the Crimson River."

"Mama, I'm scared."

"Jaron, you're a big boy, right? You will listen to Mama?"

"Yes, Mama."

"This key, you must keep it safe. Hide it. I have to hide you too—in a bad place."

"Don't cry, Mama. When will Papa and Joelle come home?"

"Papa … can't … but Joelle, I don't know. Keep the key with you always, Jaron. It will help you find home."

This time Jaron awoke at the command of the screaming pain in his right arm. "I'm dying! I'm dying! Somebody help!"

"It's time for your medicine. It'll be okay."

He drifted back to find Mama, but she'd gone. Instead, he sat huddled in the back of a truck with two children: a boy and a girl.

"I'm hungry," the boy said, eyeing the bag beside Jaron.

He pulled out the still warm loaf of bread his mama had tucked inside before she'd squeezed him one last time and then turned away. "I can share," he offered.

The girl scrunched her nose and sniffed, whimpering, "I'm hungry too."

They ate the bread together, the three of them.

"Where am I?" Jaron asked. He leaned forward, wincing at the pain radiating from his bandaged arm.

"The Infirmary," Gabria, the doctor's receptionist, answered, reaching behind him to fluff his pillow.

"How long have I been here?" he asked.

"Almost a week," she said.

"I can't remember—"

"You slept a lot. And talked. You talk in your sleep, you know."

"Oh," he said. His head thumped along with his heartbeat and he sank back into his pillow. Had he mentioned the Eradications? The shots? The fire? Did she know what he had witnessed but lacked the courage to prevent?

He stared at her face, framed in dark wispy hair, realizing it didn't matter what she knew. He knew. He was a coward, a rat-faced coward who'd stood back as two innocent people had been executed.

Why was he here? Living. Breathing. He deserved to die. "How did I hurt my arm?" he asked.

"You burned it."

He squeezed his eyes shut. So he had obeyed Captain Mar's order. "You've been looking after me?"

"I asked the doctor if I could stay with you and he agreed."

"I want to see it," he insisted suddenly, pulling at the adhesive tape.

She swatted his hand away. "You shouldn't, not yet."

"Why didn't more of me burn?" he asked, surprised he could keep the disappointment from his voice. He deserved to be punished.

Gabria answered, "After you were set ablaze someone pushed you into a water trough."

Heat crept up Jaron's face. "For the horses?"

She shook her head. "Nope! The pigs!" she told him, shaking with laughter.

"I don't see what's so funny about that."

"I'm sorry. You're right. It's not funny."

"Who would save my life?" he wondered aloud. Maybe his trainer?

"I'm not sure. Benjamin didn't say when he carried you in."

"Benjamin brought me here?"

Smiling, she said, "He stayed in the hallway all night, waiting as the doctor worked on you. He left when the doctor said you'd live."

Jaron found it hard to believe that Benjamin would care anything about what happened to him. "He must have been under orders to guard my room. He hates me."

"Maybe," Gabria admitted. "Just before he left, I saw him gulp a handful of pills and charge out of here like he was about to go off eradicating the entire countryside."

"You know what we do?" Jaron gasped.

"I know what *they* do. But you're not like them, are you?"

He didn't answer. He didn't know how. The killing made him sick, but what had he done about it? Nothing!

They sat in silence for a few moments before Gabria jumped up. "Oh! I forgot! I saved your things."

She disappeared for a few moments and then returned with a clear plastic bag containing the doctor's recording device, the knife that had killed Ansel, and the red book he'd found in Layden's kitchen.

"That's it?" he asked, his stomach feeling as though it was filled with broken glass. He reached to his neck—the key was gone! Where was it? He couldn't remember anything after Captain Mar had thrown him the matches and ordered him to burn down Layden's house.

"What's wrong, Jaron?"

Studying her face, he wondered how much she knew about him. Very possibly she knew more about his life than he did. Maybe Lord Drake had sent her here to spy on him. Maybe she'd stolen his key and was now trying to find out if he noticed or to see if it was important to him.

"Nothing's missing," he said. Was it his imagination, or did she look disappointed with his answer?

"Get some rest now. I'll be back in a little while with something to eat. You must be starved."

He clutched the bag as if he were afraid it would run away. His belongings? None of these things belonged to him. The recording device belonged to the doctor and the knife had come from Ansel's body—he loathed any claim to that. The book was Layden's. The only thing he truly owned was his key and it was missing.

Kicking off his blanket, he realized that the more he learned about the Realm of Leviathon, the more caged he was. During his years in the Heaps, he hadn't realized how his freedom had been stolen. Now he knew and he wanted to escape.

"Jaron, you look well."

He froze. "High Priestess . . . I mean, Solange," he said, reaching for his blanket to cover his legs, which were protruding from under his hospital gown.

Hide the book. The thought chimed so loud in his head that he was sure someone had spoken it aloud. He leaned to his left side and shimmied the bag under his pillow. Solange didn't seem to notice.

"What happened to it?" Solange asked.

"My arm? It was an accident. I burned it."

"Not that!" Solange said dismissively. "I mean what happened to your *key*?" Her forehead wrinkled beneath her powdered complexion, aging her under the sharp lights of the Infirmary.

"I don't know," he answered, wishing she'd shown more concern for him.

"Nurse! Nurse!" Solange yelled out the door. "Come here immediately!"

Gabria's usually rosy cheeks turned pale as she scurried into the room and encountered Solange.

"Where is the key that was around Jaron's neck?" Solange asked. "Did you take it?"

"No," Gabria said softly, her head down.

"Look at me!"

Obediently, Gabria lifted her head. "I swear I didn't take Jaron's key."

Solange opened her mouth as if to say something more and then snapped it shut and waved Gabria away. She smiled at him and he relaxed. She wasn't angry with him. Her eyes flickered mysteriously for a moment before she blanketed them with . . . kindness?

"Your mother got away," she whispered.

He exhaled, not realizing he'd even been holding his breath. "How?"

"Layden was a respected man, a leader in his community. It was better for the Enforcers to leave and let the attack be blamed on others."

"I don't understand. Who else would do that?"

"You poor boy," Solange comforted. "You spend so much time looking at the surface you don't see what's underneath."

The words were gentle and her tone soft, but Jaron caught the hinted irony.

"I have to go now," she said, dropping a jar on the table beside his bed. "Tell that nurse to put this ointment on twice a day so your burn will heal without a scar."

She slipped through the door and a moment later Gabria entered his room carrying a tray of steaming soup and soft buttered rolls.

"Why did she want a key?"

He shrugged. "I don't know. Lord Drake wants it too. I wouldn't . . . couldn't give it to *him*. But Solange . . . she's . . .

different." He stared at Gabria, "Are you sure you didn't see my key when I was brought here?"

Gabria rubbed her hands together, like she was scrubbing at an invisible spot that wouldn't come clean. "I didn't take it."

"I didn't think you did," he falsely assured her, hoping he could read her reaction to the lie he was about to give. If she had stolen it or knew where it was, maybe he could tell by some slip in her composure. "I have it hidden in a safe place."

"Really?" she said, folding her hands in her lap.

He learned nothing.

20

Riddles and Rhymes

The cream Solange left for Jaron made his arm tingle each time it was applied. After only two more weeks in the infirmary, his burn had healed enough for him to be free of the constricting bandages.

"Miraculous!" the doctor said, examining the wound. "The High Priestess has outdone herself this time. Although why she's taken such an interest in you, I have no idea." He jotted a few notes on the clipboard attached to the end of Jaron's bed. "If you keep healing at this speed, you'll be back to training within a week."

The doctor left and Jaron scrambled to the end of the bed and pulled the clipboard toward him.

IDENTITY: *Enforcer Cadet L754, a.k.a. Jaron*
HEIGHT: *173.5 cm*
WEIGHT: *62.3 kilos*
INJURY: *2nd degree burns to right arm and smoke inhalation*
PROGNOSIS: *fair excellent*
SPECIAL INSTRUCTIONS: *report all patient progress and communication to Captain Mar*

Under "Patient Treatment" there was a myriad of scrawls and abbreviations that meant nothing to Jaron. He sighed, knowing that it was useless to wish more had been written about him. He was a nobody. A Heapdweller. A number.

"Anything interesting there?" Gabria asked, carrying in a lunch tray filled with a meaty stew and thick buttered bread.

His stomach growled appreciatively at the appealing scents wafting from the tray. "Thank you," he said, sure he'd never stop being grateful for fresh food that hadn't been scavenged from the garbage.

Gabria perched on a sparsely cushioned metal chair and crossed her legs. "So what's your book about?" she asked, watching him slurp his soup.

Book? His mind went blank.

"The red book."

"Oh," he said. He'd forgotten all about it. It was still tucked under his pillow. "It's not mine. Well ... it is now, I guess."

"Did you steal it?" Gabria asked.

Jaron threw his spoon down. "No! I was protecting it and then it was given to me by ... someone."

"Do you know how to read?"

He scooped up another spoonful of stew, annoyed. Did she think he was stupid just because he grew up in the Heaps? "I can read," he said finally after swallowing his food.

"Why don't you read it now, then? It might be something important," she said before jumping up and exiting the room.

Savouring the rest of the stew, he dipped the bread into the amber gravy. This food tasted even better than what the Enforcers ate in the mess hall. After eating, he set the tray aside and reached under his pillow to draw out the plastic bag.

The doctor's recording device plummeted onto the bed. He pressed play, trying to remember the last meal he had recorded. He heard a "thunk" and then listened, horrified, to Layden's gentle voice saying, "They forced you to do it. It's only a house filled with things. It's the people that make it a home."

Jaron fumbled to turn off the recorder before the thunder of blasting bullets made him relive the horror of that day. He held his finger above the erase button but couldn't follow through. He didn't deserve to clear the evidence of his shameful act.

He slipped the recorder back into the bag, carefully avoiding the knife. This bag was a record of the blood that stained his hands—Ansel's, Layden's, and Layden's wife.

Retrieving the book, he stared at it. His hand traced the shape of the key embedded in the cover. *The Ancient Way.* What did it mean? He supposed the only way to find the answers would be to follow Gabria's advice and read it.

Breathlessly flipping through the pages, he stopped as a slip of paper fluttered out. He picked it up and read the handwritten note:

> *For Jaron and Joelle,*
> > *May you find your way to the land of promise.*
> > *There you will find home.*
>
> > > > *In Love and Hope,*
> > > > *Mama and Papa*

Jaron and Joelle. With his heart hammering an uneven rhythm, the book slid from his hands. How had Layden come into possession of this book? Was the Realm really so small that a book originally intended for him would find its way back into his hands? He traced his name. Jaron. *And Joelle,* he thought, and her face appeared again in his memory—a child laughing, her golden hair tugged back in a pink bow with curls spilling down.

Leafing through the pages of the book, he stopped to read here and there but the words made no sense. It was a book of riddles and he had no idea what the passages meant.

In frustration, he skipped to the final page and the words leapt up, commanding his attention. The verse was titled "*The Way Home.*"

He read:

> *The heart determines the path.*
> *The Ancient Crimson River traverses the Mountain.*
> *Only the one transformed by the sacrifice of love*
> *Holds the key to Home.*

Underneath was a penciled message, obviously written in haste: *Jaron holds the key, and Joelle, the book.*

"Jaron holds the key," he whispered, reaching to his neck automatically, forgetting his loss. Finding no familiar metal shape, he slammed the book shut. Why bother reading any more? He'd lost the key, his only chance of finding a home.

"Was it interesting?" Gabria asked, smiling as she returned to collect his tray of dirty dishes.

He studied her face, wishing he knew how to read people like words on a page. He needed help. If only Ansel weren't dead…

"I had a friend once," he said, ignoring her question. "He was the only person I've ever trusted."

"Ah," she said, sitting on the end of his bed. "You're trying to decide if you should trust me also."

He sat there, weighing his decision. He'd learned so much about the Realm of Leviathon since leaving the Heaps. There was nothing, no one, untouched by deceit or suspicion. His doubt ran so deep that he wondered if he would even dare to trust Ansel if it were possible to see him again. *Yes you would*, he told himself, ashamed that he might be tempted to so easily forget Ansel's selfless act and grieved that there would never be another meeting with such a friend.

"Read the last page," he said, passing the book to her.

She read it aloud and the words took on new meaning as he heard her speak.

"Only the one changed by the sacrifice of love holds the key to home," he repeated thoughtfully.

"Do you understand what it means?" she asked.

"My friend . . . he died. It should have been me," Jaron said. "Don't you get it? He sacrificed himself."

"Tell me what happened," she whispered, moving closer to him.

The words spilled out like an unstoppable rain, starting with Ansel's death in the ring and Lord Drake's desire for the key and ending with Layden's dying plea. Gabria's gentle prodding questions pulled more information from him than he had intended to share.

"Where did you hide the key?" she asked, her face solemn, waiting.

He hesitated. Why was she so curious? Was she trying to get her hands on the key too? Blinking, he stared into her blue eyes, feeling unbalanced for suspecting everyone of treachery.

"A safe place," he lied.

"So you won't even tell me?"

"Not . . . no," he answered, wishing he really had hidden the key somewhere safe. He was torn between anger at himself for losing it and resentment at ever having it in the first place. *Keep the key with you always*, Mama had said in his dream. What good had it done? It had made him vulnerable—a target for Lord Drake.

Gabria slathered more ointment on his fading burns. As Jaron watched her work, her lips moved.

"What are you whispering?" he asked.

She pulled her hands away. "I was speaking a cur . . . a blessing," she stuttered. "For . . . your health."

"What's that?"

"It's when you ask for something important."

"Who were you asking?"

"Someone more powerful than I am," she answered, and then she collected the lunch tray and scurried away.

What was she talking about? Someone more powerful? There was no one else there except for the two of them.

He stared at the final verse in the book and inhaled slowly, a pang of regret gnawing at his stomach. Why had he divulged so much about Ansel to her?

What did it matter now? he argued with himself. Ansel had wasted his sacrifice anyway. Jaron hadn't changed. He was still cowering, cautiously obeying whatever force was stronger. All hope of finding home was gone. He possessed the book but had lost the key. What good was the one without the other?

"Joelle," he whispered, wondering why he hadn't remembered she was his *sister* until his brush with death. Now he knew what his dream of Mama meant. She had told him that Papa would never come back. He must have been eradicated in his quest to find a better place—home. But what about Joelle. Was she still alive?

This book had found its way back to Jaron through Layden. He couldn't imagine that the man sobbing in the dirt had ever harmed anyone. Maybe he'd found it somewhere—next to Papa's dead body?

And who would have murdered Papa? The Enforcers, of course. And now he had been ordered to kill his mother to become one of them. Lord Drake and his Enforcers were a killing machine that never stopped.

"I won't do it," he said through clenched teeth.

His arm itched and he glanced down at it. The burns had almost disappeared! What had the doctor said? Miraculous? How had Solange's cream cured him so quickly? His skin tingled and he watched as the last traces of the burn vanished.

"I won't eradicate my mother—or Layden's daughter. Whoever she is, I won't kill anyone!" he said firmly. "This time I won't be a coward."

Grabbing the book, Ansel's knife, and the voice recorder, Jaron slipped from his room into the hallway in search of suitable clothing. After all, he couldn't seek out the High Priestess of Leviathon in a hospital gown.

He discovered a closet filled with clean, folded Cadet uniforms. Dressing quickly, he worked out his plan to slip into the castle and find Solange. He'd beg her to help him save this Freesia from Lord Drake in exchange for his key.

The key he no longer had.

21

The River's End

For days upon days the memory of her parents' dead bodies in front of the smoking ruins of their home had been her constant companion. She could still envision the blood that stained their clothing. While awake, a fog cloaked her and she breathed under the shadow of death. While asleep, the shadow stalked her nightmares.

"Mama!" she had screamed days ago, running across her yard. She'd reached out and then stopped. She couldn't bear to touch her mother's lifeless body.

She'd stumbled to the charred doorstep, scorching her hand as she grabbed at the railing, which then crumpled into a hissing mound of live coals. Immune to the sunlight, she had walked away blindly, engulfed in the memory of her mother's and father's vacant stares.

I'm alone, she thought now, still drifting through the fog.

Voices encircled her, swarming, but she swatted them away. *I'll listen tomorrow*, she told herself, but the voices grew louder, angrier, buzzing around her head.

"Run to the river!" someone screamed, shoving her.

She felt stinging jolts zap her face, her arms. The pain threatened to break through the fog. Someone tugged at her arm and she lurched forward as the stinging spread to her neck and scalp.

The icy water made her gasp as a hand plunged her head under the surface and held it there. She choked, expelling air as she was forced to stay submerged. Mercifully, the buzzing subsided and the pain in her body soothed beneath the water's surface.

Stillness.

And then it was as if the water spoke to her. *Breathe me in and float away,* the water whispered. *You'll be at peace.*

She opened her mouth, desperate to obey, but before she could inhale the water's welcome solitude she was plucked from its grip and thrown to the ground.

Someone pounded on her chest, yelling at her to breathe.

Let me go to Papa, she tried to say as air was forced into her mouth.

"Breathe!" someone screamed again.

I know that voice, she thought, warming as if the sun had broken through. *It's okay, Papa. I'll stay here for now.*

The fog parted as her eyes focused. "Riak," she whispered. For a moment, the shadow lifted.

"Are you alright?" he said, pulling her close. "You must have at least twenty stings."

"Stings?" Freesia said, struggling to lift her arms, which were peppered with angry red welts.

"You stumbled into a hornets' nest. We all did."

"Did you get stung too?"

"A few times. And Devora got three or four. But you got the worst of it."

"Devora?" Freesia asked, glancing toward the river where the other girl stood alone. Her memories flooded back, the shadow threatening to overwhelm her again. "My parents!" she sobbed.

"Try not to think about it," Riak soothed as he coated her stings with river mud and then wrapped a blanket around her shaking shoulders.

She squeezed her eyes shut. "Don't hide the truth from me, Riak. I know they were killed because of me."

"Don't...you couldn't have known what Lord Drake would do. Nobody could."

Freesia looked toward Devora. "Did she tell you why I left the Maternity Program?"

He nodded.

"What am I going to do? I have no one."

He pulled her to her feet. "That's not true. You have me...always."

Devora walked towards them, her hand resting on her belly. "We need to keep moving," she urged, glancing down the river. "Once they find our trail, we're dead."

Freesia tugged the blanket closer. "I never dreamed Lord Drake would be cruel enough to have my parents murdered. He's always making proclamations to bestow favours on the loyal subjects of the Realm."

"Now we know what happens to the subjects who are considered disloyal," Riak said.

"My parents weren't disloyal," she said bitterly. "I was."

Silently, the three of them plodded further along the river. Freesia had never been this far north before. "Do you know where we are?" she asked.

Riak shook his head. "No. We've been walking for almost two weeks now and I've only ever travelled as far as two days north when I was hunting elk."

"Your parents won't know what happened to you," she said, now feeling responsible for ruining his life too. And maybe even Devora's—surely the Matron wouldn't *really* have sent the girl away *just* for being pregnant. Then she remembered the scene at her parents' farm, realizing that beyond the civil exterior of the Realm there lurked unbelievable cruelty. Both she and Devora were better off now. But not Riak. He still had a home.

"After I found you, my father found us. He said he'd … take care of them … your parents."

She closed her eyes, chasing a fragile dream. "I watched Papa bury him," she mumbled.

"Freesia!" Riak shook her. "What's she taking about?" he said, looking to Devora.

"I don't know. Maybe she means her brother. She told me he died."

"A brother?" Riak said. "I didn't know you had a brother."

"Not my brother," she said, the memory fading fast. "A man." The setting sun illuminated her fair hair. "Thank you both for helping me," she said. "And I am grateful to your father for honouring my parents." Straightening her shoulders back, she added, "We should keep going. All of this will be for nothing if we get caught."

"I think we should eat and then rest until first light tomorrow," Riak suggested. "The terrain's getting more difficult to navigate."

"I am starving," Freesia agreed.

Riak unpacked his supply of gathered berries and leftover roasted wild turkey. "I only light a fire to cook under the cover of the morning mist," he explained. "You haven't been eating since …"

"… my parents," she whispered, wondering how she had drifted so long in her own world of broken memories.

Devora ate by the river, then stood aloof while Freesia and Riak arranged themselves for sleeping.

"Lie down, Devora, you *must* be exhausted," Freesia insisted.

"I'm fine," the other girl answered, finally perching on a rock as if ready to take off at a moment's notice.

"Suit yourself," Freesia mumbled, drifting off to sleep.

The next day, they arose early before the sun. Splashing river water over her skin, Freesia could almost imagine reclining in the atrium and delighting in the soft gurgle of the water bubbling over the artificial stones of the fountain. She felt ashamed of longing for comfort that came at such a price. "Did you rest at all?" she asked Devora.

"I leaned against the rock," Devora said, also rubbing the icy water over her face, "but I couldn't sleep. The minute my eyes would close, I'd hear a coyote howl." She pressed her hand against her side.

"Are you alright?"

"I'm fine!" Devora snapped. "My stomach pinches tight once in a while, but it doesn't hurt. I can keep up, don't worry."

"We have to go," Riak said.

Massaging her own side, Freesia nodded. The stony riverbed was a far cry from the feather mattresses at the Maternity Ward. "I guess we're both a little stiff today."

They trudged on slowly. Freesia wondered if escape would even be possible at such a snail's pace. Midmorning, the ground changed from smooth pebbles to steep, jagged crags covered with slick moss. The spray of foamy rapids spewing dark water over the river rocks served to underscore a growing sense of danger.

"I'll go first," Devora said, gripping a stunted tree branch to help stabilize her footing. Her efforts were wasted and she slid to the ground, landing with a noticeable thud.

"Wait! Let me help," Riak said, boosting her up over the wall of slimy boulders.

Devora broke free of Riak's grip and struggled to her feet on top of the rocks. "Oh, no!"

"What is it?" Riak asked, his voice strained.

"We'll never make it past!" Devora wailed. Standing like a statue, she pointed ahead.

Riak gripped Freesia's hand. "What's wrong?" he asked. "Is someone up there?"

Fear stabbed at Freesia's heart. *They're here—we've been caught!*

"No," Devora said, dropping her arm and staring down at them. "Come see for yourselves."

Riak pushed Freesia up over the rocks, steadying her as her footing gave way on a moss-covered stone. His touch strengthened her resolve. They would be safe. Somehow, they would find a way.

Reaching the top, she finally understood why Devora's dark skin had paled despite the sun's glow. None of them had ever travelled this far. No one had ever seen a map of the Northern Territory—it was forbidden. If they had, they might have known how impossible a task would lay before them.

The mountain loomed as far to the east and west as one could fathom, appearing to be an impossible barrier to their freedom. "We should turn back," Freesia said, finally saying what she figured everyone must be thinking.

They had followed the Gauntlet for nothing!

"We can't," Riak said, setting his lips together. "There has to be a way forward. We already know there's nothing left back there." He swung his arm back, pointing down the river.

He was right. Their future was north, or nothing.

Devora stumbled along beside them, her breathing becoming laboured in the afternoon sun.

"You should have slept last night, Devora. This journey's too hard for you." Freesia reached for Riak's hand and allowed him to pull her along the twisting riverbed.

"You'd like me to stop, wouldn't you? You think I'll slow you down—when we reach the mountain. You'll leave me behind, won't you? You know I can't climb," Devora accused.

"What are you talking about?" Freesia said, staring at Devora's curled lips. "What kind of people do you think we are?"

"People!" Devora spat. "Jaron, Benjamin, Solange. They're all the same. *You're* all the same. You stand alone!"

"Nobody's being left alone," Riak said. "We'll keep going as far as we can. Then we'll figure out what to do next. Together!"

The tempo of the river thundered like an erratic drumbeat, adding to Freesia's growing agitation with Devora's accusation. It wasn't fair! She had done nothing but help the stupid girl even when she, herself, had lost everything!

"There's another bend up ahead," Riak observed. "We're at the base of the mountain, but the river goes further!"

The riverbank narrowed and the three of them slipped into single file. Freesia barely glanced at Devora, but even still, she could feel the angry stare burning into the back of her neck.

When the pathway widened, Freesia lifted her head and took in the wonder of the deep pool catching the cascading water spilling from the mountain. Here, at the base of the waterfall, the river ended abruptly. Devora moaned and collapsed to the ground.

Freesia ran to her side and pulled on her arm. "You can't give up now! We'll find a passage through the mountain. There has to be a way!"

Devora clutched her stomach. "It hurts," she cried out.

Freesia's heart dropped when she realized that the dark wet spot on, Devora's dress had not come from the river's spray. She knew a little about the birthing process from books she'd read in the Maternity Ward, but not enough to be useful—especially not here, away from doctors and a medical facility.

"What's wrong?" Riak asked, now trying to help raise Devora to her feet.

"Let her be. She's not going anywhere."

"What are you talking about? We can't just leave her here alone."

Freesia sank to the ground, her skin burning beneath caked mud and the noonday heat. "Of course we're not leaving her here alone!" she said. "Her water just broke. Devora's having her baby! And it's too soon."

22

Unwelcome Night

"I can't do this!"

"You have to, Devora. I see the baby's head," Riak said.

"What happens if I don't?" she panted.

"Then the baby dies."

Devora breathed deeply, released momentarily from the grip of a contraction. What did she care if the baby died?

She saw Freesia studying her face. "Tell her the rest, Riak," Freesia said firmly.

"Freesia!" Riak cautioned. "I don't want to scare her."

"She needs to know the rest or she won't push."

The wave of pain washed over her again and Devora's whole body trembled. She held on to Freesia's hand, squeezing it but still refusing to push. Freesia was right. She didn't care. This thing had caused her enough anguish. Let it die. She'd been hoping to find a doctor to help her extract the pregnancy anyway, but their pilgrimage north had erased that possibility.

The contraction broke and Riak said, "You have to push because if you don't, you'll die too."

"Arghhh!" she roared. He would pay for this! She pictured Jaron's face in front of her as she pushed with all the force of her hatred, certain she'd split in two. It was only seven new moons since he'd ripped her world apart and left her used and broken.

"Once more!" Riak yelled.

She obeyed.

"It's a girl." Riak placed the scrawny bundle in Devora's arms. It was no bigger than a rat. The thing squirmed and then opened its mouth and screeched.

"Take it away," she said, passing the creature to Freesia. There, she was done! She tried to get up and her ears rang as nausea seized her stomach and the world turned black.

She awoke to a damp cloth on her forehead. "You need to rest," Freesia told her.

"We have to go," Devora said weakly. "Just leave that thing here. It'll slow us down."

"What's she talking about?" Riak demanded. "What kind of a monster is she? The baby's so tiny—only a couple pounds. How could she even think of leaving it?"

"Shh, let her rest, Riak. You don't know how bad things were for her. She raised herself in the Garbage Heaps. She doesn't know how to care for anyone but herself."

"You should have left her behind at the medical facility."

Devora stiffened, waiting to hear Freesia's response. Is that what they would decide to do to her now? Leave her behind with that stupid Screaming Bundle? Fine! When the dogs tracked her down, she'd throw it to them, distracting the animals long enough for her own escape. But even as she had the thought the baby whimpered, like a muted plea for mercy.

"I brought her with me because I needed her help," Freesia said.

Selfish rat, Devora thought.

"And she needed mine," Freesia continued.

Oh.

"Look after the baby while I try to find a way out of here," Riak said.

"I don't know what to do!" Freesia protested. "You're the one with five brothers and sisters! And the baby's so small—I don't think she's breathing right."

"Keep her warm and feed her. I'm not sure if her lungs are strong enough . . . anyway, see if you can get Devora to nurse her," he said, walking away.

"Devora," Freesia whispered gently. "You have to try and feed the baby now. She's hungry."

"You do it," Devora said, keeping her eyes closed.

"I can't."

"Why not?" Devora asked, turning toward her and gesturing toward the river. "Just give it some river water and a few of those berries you gathered."

Freesia stared down at her.

"What?" Devora said, yawning.

"Don't you know how babies eat?"

"Of course I do! With their mouths, the same way we do."

"No they don't," Freesia said, and she went on to explain further.

"You're kidding!" Devora sputtered. "I'm not going to feed the thing at all, then! Just put it down over there. It'll stop wailing eventually. The Five-Years in the Heaps always did."

Freesia gripped the baby, now cozy in a blanket. "You feed this baby or else we'll leave you here for the Enforcers to find," she threatened, depositing the infant in Devora's arms.

"Fine! I'll try," Devora said, yanking the Squealing Bundle close to her chest. "But it better figure out how to do it by itself because I'm not helping it."

The baby nestled next to Devora, quieting after a few moments. She decided it was still a scrawny little thing, but maybe it wasn't as ugly as she first thought. "I don't think it's hungry."

She must have dozed off again herself, because when she opened her eyes it was dusk and Freesia was pacing nearby with Riak's pack hoisted on her shoulder.

"What's wrong?" Devora asked. Were they sneaking away without her? Panic robbed her of her breath.

"Riak isn't back yet. He's been gone for hours."

Devora relaxed. "Maybe he just hasn't found a passageway yet."

Freesia shook her head. "He promised to be back in two hours. Something's wrong."

Feeling pressure against her chest, Devora glanced down to find the baby with its eyes closed, sucking on her breast. Suddenly, a tiny fist clamped around Devora's thumb, displaying a scarlet heart-shaped birthmark on the little one's hand. Her eyes stung with tears as she watched the infant struggle to eat. She and her baby were alike: imperfect and driven to survive. "What should we do?"

"I don't know. If he's hurt, we should find him."

The air was chilled and damp. Devora shivered. "What if he's not hurt? What if he just took off and left us?"

"He wouldn't do that to me!"

"How do you know? I never dreamed Jaron would do what he did."

"Riak's not like Jaron! He grew up in a civilized world, not like—" she stopped, her face turning red.

"Not in the Garbage Heaps like me," Devora finished.

"That's not what I meant." Freesia lowered the pack and sank down to the ground. "But it doesn't matter now, does it? We're still here together, running away from the same thing."

Devora's heart thudded. "We have nowhere left to go, do we?"

"I don't know," Freesia said. "All I could think of when I escaped from the program was reaching home, but now that's gone. Everything's gone. And now something's happened to Riak!"

A noise from the forest alerted them to Riak's approach.

"He's back!" Freesia said, sighing as she stood up to greet him.

He emerged from the forest, his grim face illuminated briefly by the sunset's fiery farewell. Freesia gasped. "Who?"

"Benjamin!" Devora whispered, her heart leaping.

23
Truth or Lies

"Jaron! Wait!"

A chill shot its way up his spine.

"You can't leave without the doctor's permission," Gabria said, cornering him in the hallway.

He stared past her toward the exit doors. He'd almost made it.

"I'm fine, really. My arm's completely better and I'm just going back to the barracks," he said, forcing himself to speak calmly, hoping she wouldn't notice the anxious pitch in his voice.

"Let me see your arm," she ordered, grabbing his arm and pushing back the sleeve of his shirt. "Amazing!" she said, running her fingers over his perfect skin. "But you still can't be released without seeing the doctor first."

"I saw him … just now," Jaron sputtered.

Gabria hung on to his arm, trapping him. He'd trusted her enough to share the details of his life, but now he felt as if she'd become his enemy. She wasn't very strong, he mused, thinking of the rope he'd seen in the closet of uniforms where he'd changed. He could overpower her.

"You're not going back to the barracks, are you?" she asked.

He shook his head. "How did you guess?"

"Your eyes. You don't lie very well."

165

Worry nagged at him. Did she know he had lied about the key too? "I won't eradicate my mother to become one of them," he said, deciding to throw an element of the truth between them.

"If you refuse, Lord Drake will have you executed. You know that."

"I don't care." He wondered if he dared try to lie once more. "Besides," he said, turning away so she couldn't see his eyes. "I have something Lord Drake wants."

"What?" She grabbed his arm again and dug her fingers into his flesh.

"My key, remember?"

"You have it with you now?" she asked.

Shaking his head, Jaron smiled. "No. It's somewhere safe until I need it. I'm going to offer it to Solange in exchange for her help to save my mother."

Did he imagine it, or did Gabria relax her grip?

"I'll help you," she said. "I know how to find Solange."

"You know where she is?"

Her eyes widened. "Oh no!" she protested. "I only know that she is usually at Lord Drake's castle in the evenings for parties. At least, that's what the newspapers say."

"Why would you help me?"

"You can guess the answer to that!"

"I remind you of someone you used to care about," he offered.

She nodded.

"And for that, you'd risk your life?" he asked, doubting her, yet longing for her assistance. Maybe he should tell her that he really had nothing to exchange after all.

"Yes," she said. And guiding him toward the stairs, they slipped through a seldom-used side entrance that led to the outskirts of the compound. "I have a confession to make," she said as they hastened away, ducking behind the lengthening shadows cast by the afternoon light.

Jaron quickened his pace.

"Don't you want to know what it is?" she asked, matching her stride to his.

He shrugged. Words or deeds no longer held the power to shock him. She had offered to help, and here she was. If that had changed and she was now prepared to betray him, he'd deal with it. Saving his own life held no appeal anymore. Besides, he had his own secrets.

"I read your book."

"That's your confession?"

"I wanted you to know. I thought you could tell me what the verses mean because I didn't understand a thing! I figured you *must* know what it's all about. After all, your name's written in it."

"Sorry to disappoint you, but when I read it like you suggested, it meant nothing to me either. Except for that last page we read together."

Gabria held out her hand, "May I see it again for a moment?"

Don't give it to her, he thought and then shook off the unbidden warning. She'd already read it. What difference did it make now? Slipping the note out from inside the cover, he passed her the book. Some things were too sacred to share.

"Did you notice this part yet?" she asked, pointing to a verse in the middle of the book.

He stopped beside her as she read aloud:

> *The burning rod illuminates the darkness,*
> *The sting of death is lifted, reversing the first curse,*
> *Releasing the key into the hand of the door.*

"What do you think it means?" she asked. "It's the only other verse in here that mentions the key."

Tucking the note into his trouser pocket, he gazed at her as if seeing her for the first time. "You've spent a lot of time thinking about this, haven't you? Is that all you did while I was unconscious?"

"I wanted to learn why Solange and Lord Drake have so desperately wanted your key. But it doesn't matter now, does it? You're going to give it to them even though it has some sort of power to reverse a curse."

Liar, he accused himself. She was risking her life to help him sneak into Lord Drake's castle, all the while believing his fabrication. "I don't even know what a curse is. Do you?" he asked.

As if not hearing his question, she turned the pages. "This book *must* have been meant for you," she said, pointing to his name penciled inside the cover. "But who is Joelle?"

"My sister."

Gabria sucked in her breath. "You have a sister? Where is she?"

"I'm not sure," he said, trying to stir up the image of the girl with curls of spun gold. "I thought maybe she was dead ... but now, I think I know where she is."

"Where?" Gabria snapped the book shut.

He paused, doubting his nagging hunch. Maybe he belonged in the same insane ward his mother had supposedly escaped from—the idea seemed too crazy to be possible.

"Where is your sister?" she asked again, her voice terse.

"Trapped in the palace with Lord Drake," he replied, sharing his wild imaginations. *None of it seemed believable, but the blond curls ...*

The sun splashed its final blushing glory across the sapphire sky and its rays danced in Gabria's eyes. "You mean Solange," she whispered.

"That's the real reason why I'm going to her now. I haven't even dared to admit it to myself. But I'm convinced she's Joelle. Once I rescue her, together we'll find ... save our mother."

Pushing forward with renewed hope, he now understood what force had driven him to the castle. Not some misguided notion that Layden's daughter, Freesia, was his mother, but the subconscious belief that he'd found his sister.

Freesia retreated into the shadows as the stranger in uniform strode into the clearing beside the waterfall. Shifting his gun, his eyes darted toward the infant in Devora's arms.

"What's that thing?" he asked, his expression vacant.

What is wrong with him? Freesia wondered as he blinked repeatedly as if he couldn't focus on a moving target.

"Benjamin! It's me. How did you know where to find me?" Devora cried out, struggling to get up.

"Stand back!" he ordered, whipping his gun into position and flexing his fingers next to the trigger.

Devora halted, staring at him with eyes that resembled a wounded animal, confused and alone.

"Let me hold her." Freesia took the baby from Devora's limp arms and whispered, "Look at his uniform. He's an Enforcer."

"It's okay." Devora mumbled in a pleading voice as she stumbled toward him. "He's Benjamin, my friend. You remember me, right?"

Benjamin. The least repulsive of Devora's two Heapdweller friends.

"You need to come with me," Benjamin demanded.

"I don't understand," Devora cried, grabbing his arm. "Look at me! It's Devora!"

He shook free of her grip and Freesia held her breath. Then it was as if he'd finally heard Devora for the first time. Lowering his gun, he stepped toward her. "I know who you are, you rat-faced traitor," he said, his voice dripping with contempt.

Devora crumpled up like a rag doll flung to the ground.

He lifted his head and stared with glassy eyes. "And who are you?"

"Freesia," she answered, tasting salt as she licked her parched lips.

Baring his teeth—half-grin, half-growl—he said, "You're both coming with me."

With knees like jelly, Freesia stepped forward, trying to pass the baby back to Devora.

"No!" Benjamin commanded. "That's staying behind! Put it down."

"But—"

Crack! He slammed his gun across Freesia's cheek.

She swayed, blackness threatening to consume her. Then she steadied, but her stomach still churned with nausea until she gagged. The baby whimpered.

With no time to find a sheltered nook, she hastily shoved the swaddled infant into a niche in the cliff. *Come back soon, Riak, and find her before it's too late,* she pleaded silently.

Benjamin tilted his head sideways, squinting his eyes. "So you're Freesia?" he said. "You look too young to be Jaron's mother."

24

The Belly of Leviathon

Spiked spires loomed ahead. The silhouette of the castle was a menacing apparition against the moonlit backdrop and Jaron wondered how the castle would appear in the daylight. Then he remembered the papers he'd scavenged in the Heaps. Shiny colour photographs had been accompanied by the words, "Lord Drake invites loyal citizens of the Realm for picnics in his sprawling gardens where they are served teacakes and lemonade under cloudless skies."

How could the citizens of the Realm not know what their leader was really like? Jaron puzzled at this, despising, yet envying them for their ignorance—or was it pretended ignorance?

"We'll never get past the gate," he said to Gabria as they hid, camouflaged amongst a clump of bushes to avoid the scrutiny of security lights crisscrossing the courtyard.

"I know another way … a secret passage," she told him.

He grabbed her arm. "What are you talking about?"

How did she know so much? Was she leading him into a trap? Maybe he should have tied her up back at the barracks after all and found his own way to the castle.

"I mean, I know *of* one. I heard the … the … *doctor* mention it!"

"Why would the doctor need to enter the castle through a secret passage?" Jaron asked. But he relaxed his grip on her arm.

"I think it has something to do with Solange and her . . . rituals," she whispered, pulling him deeper into the shadows.

"What does she do?" he whispered back.

"She's the High Priestess."

"I know that!" Jaron snapped. "But I have no idea what that means! What does Lord Drake make her do?" He remembered Solange's eyes searching for him as she waltzed. Was Solange actually a prisoner?

"She speaks the words of Leviathon," Gabria said, her tone hardening.

Jaron shivered as an icy breeze brushed across him. Gabria sounded angry, but at whom? Lord Drake?

She led him deeper into the forest until they stood before a wall of solid rock. "The entrance is here somewhere, hidden from view," she said, poking and prodding the surface. "There's supposed to be a loose stone."

"I'll help," he offered, running his fingers along the jagged rocks, unsure of what he was looking for.

"Dirty rat!" Gabria cursed suddenly, shaking her hand.

Stunned, Jaron stared at her. "You sound just like a Heapdweller!" he said.

"I do not!" she said, wincing. She sucked the blood from her finger.

He hurried to her side. "What happened?" He examined her hand in the moonlight.

"What do you think? I cut it on the stupid rock," she complained, yanking her hand back and sticking her finger in her mouth again to stop the bleeding. "I'll be fine! Just keep looking for the stone!"

He moved closer to where she'd been searching, testing each section of the rock. Finally one wiggled. "I think I've found it!" he announced.

"Pull it towards you."

He tugged until the stone sprung out as if it were attached to a lever. Within a split-second, the ground trembled beneath his feet and a large section of the rock swung inward, revealing a dark passageway. Dread slithered around him, its coils compressing him until he thought his lungs would explode. He couldn't move forward into the darkness. It was time to leave, escape—find somewhere, someplace, that Lord Drake did not control.

"Hold my electric torch," Gabria said, awkwardly digging in her shirt pocket with her uninjured hand. "I brought this just in case we needed it, but so far the moon has shone bright enough."

"You've been here before, haven't you?" Flashing the beam toward her, he hoped the light would reflect the truth.

"Yes. Once."

"I should have never trusted you!" Jaron threw the torch to the ground and the light extinguished.

Gabria retrieved it and flicked the switch on once again. "I'm sorry I didn't tell you before. I swore I'd never reveal the secret passage after the doctor brought me here to help treat a patient. But you know now ... everything."

Her soothing voice reminded Jaron he wasn't alone. Slowly the tentacles of fear relaxed their grip and he could breathe again. "I'd never have found my way without you," he said. "I'm sorry I doubted you."

"Forget it. Besides, I wanted to come for my own reasons. I want to see an end to the reigning powers in Leviathon as much as you do." She brushed his cheek with her lips. "Together, we'll find her."

Jaron led the way and they descended down roughly chiselled stone stairs, sinking into the musty depths of the earth until they reached a lengthy passage heading in the direction of the castle. *It must go underneath the pit of snakes in the chasm below the drawbridge*, he thought, shuddering as his mind echoed the imaginary hiss of venomous mouths.

"Lord Drake has to know about this secret passage. Why doesn't he post a guard?"

"I don't know," Gabria said, falling behind.

He waited for her to catch up. "Is your hand feeling better?"

"A little."

"Maybe Solange will have more of that cream that cured my burn."

"Maybe," she muttered.

Pressing forward, Jaron listened as the crunch of their footsteps mingled with the gentle trickle of dripping water. Gabria was humming, almost chanting, to the rhythm of their steps. His shoulders relaxed and his breathing settled into a slow, steady pace as his eyelids grew heavy. He stopped moving and she crashed into him.

"What's wrong?" Gabria asked. "Why did you stop?" Her voice sounded harsh in contrast to her soothing chant.

"It's peaceful here," Jaron said sleepily. "I wanted to enjoy it for a moment."

She brushed past him. "This is no time for peace," she hissed. "It's time to save your sister, remember?"

Guiltily, he stumbled after her. She was right. He'd been controlled by fear for so long that the seductive aura of calm had swept in and stolen his resolve. He blinked his eyes and shook his head to clear the haze that had settled around him. Remembering where he was, he surged forward through the underbelly of the Realm of Leviathon, hoping he wouldn't encounter any deadly serpents until after he'd saved Joelle.

"I think this is it," Gabria said as the tunnel ended without warning.

The etched wood of the door resembled the ancient drawbridge Jaron had seen spanning the chasm on the night of Benjamin's graduation.

Gabria twisted the rusted knob and thrust her shoulder against the door. "It won't budge," she moaned, sinking down on the stone floor.

"Let me try." Jaron's entire life had been governed by doors and keys. This door was *not* going to stop him! He kicked at it with his steel-toed boots and splinters flew. "Open up, you stupid thing!" he screamed, kicking it again.

"You're going to hurt yourself," she said.

"I don't care," he roared, his chest heaving as he gulped the sour air of the tunnel.

And he didn't care, not in this moment of reckless red-hot anger when he felt like he could take on the whole world and win. "I don't care if the entire tunnel collapses on our heads!"

Gabria stared up at him from the floor, her lips moving. *How could she sit there as if nothing mattered?* he thought. What was wrong with her?

What was wrong with *him?*

He paced in the passageway, longing to see the vastness of the stars up above. No matter how much his world expanded, his freedom continually diminished. Maybe his existence in the Garbage Heaps—living under the open sky with only the barest necessities for survival—was the most autonomy he'd ever know.

"We will succeed," Gabria said calmly, patting the ground. "Sit. Rest."

He slumped down beside her, close enough to hear her quiet, steady chant. His wild heartbeat gradually resumed an unhurried tempo and his breathing settled into a lazy, shallow rhythm. "We have to find another way into the castle," he mumbled.

Gabria smiled, sighing. "Don't worry, Jaron, it'll be fine."

Tap, tap, tap echoed a sound from somewhere behind the door.

"What's that noise?" he whispered, suddenly more alert. He blinked, trying to focus. The stale air in the tunnel was affecting him strangely.

She shrugged. "Footsteps?"

From the other side of the door, metal scratched against metal in the lock and soon the handle began to turn. He held his breath.

The lock clicked and the heavy door swung back silently.

"Welcome, Jaron," the High Priestess said, her face illuminated.

"Solange." He breathed, inhaling her presence like oxygen. He needed her and here she was.

Gabria rose to her feet, standing beside him.

"This is my nurse ... my friend, Gabria. I think you saw her in the Infirmary," Jaron said, introducing his companion to Solange.

"Gabria," Solange said, reaching to touch the nurse's injured hand. "You're hurt."

"Yes, Solange," Gabria replied, bowing to the High Priestess.

"Poor dear," Solange said. "Go to the herb room and soak your hand in a pan of warm water steeped with blackroot. It's by the cauldron where we mix potions."

"Of course," Gabria said, stepping through the door.

"Gabria, wait!" Jaron gasped. "How do you know where to go?"

Solange reached out and touched his cheek. "Poor Jaron, so confused. Now let *me* introduce Gabria, my apprentice, to you."

Gabria swirled around and curtsied to Jaron with a smirk on her face and his mouth felt like he'd swallowed sand. "Your apprentice?" he croaked.

Solange laughed, her brassy curls bouncing on her shoulders. "Gabria's the best Interrogator in the Realm, a reclaimed rat from the Garbage Heaps, just like you." She patted Gabria on the arm. "Off you go, dear. I'll get the details from you later. Right now you take care of that hand."

Gabria nodded. "I will," she said, "but there's one thing I have to tell you now or I'll just burst!"

Jaron waited, already feeling as if he'd been punched in the gut.

"He thinks . . . he thinks you're his sister, Joelle!" she said, choking with laughter.

Solange turned to him. "Really?" she said smugly. "How wonderful! Perhaps you're even more stupid than I first thought."

He lowered his eyes, ashamed he'd failed so completely. His only consolation was that he had found out about Solange's true character without turning over his key. Wherever it was, he desperately hoped it would stay hidden from the deceitful grasp of the High Priestess.

"You're not imprisoned by Lord Drake," he said, stunned by her altered appearance in the shadowy light. She seemed . . . older.

"How right you are," she said, clapping her hands together. "Lord Drake belongs to me. He's traded his life to Leviathon in exchange for the riches of the Realm."

"Leviathon?"

"Stupid boy," she hissed. "Haven't you figured it out yet? Look at your book, on the first page."

He opened *The Ancient Way*, hating that Solange and Gabria seemed to know more about the contents of the book than he did.

"Read it," she ordered.

He read, his hands shaking as he held the book:

The one, the underlord of the Realm, Leviathon,
steals the children from their Home,
cursing them and their offspring until they cry out for death.
And still, in death he grips them—until the words herein are
*   fulfilled,*
and the first curse is reversed.

"Ansel," he breathed. "I wish you were here to fight beside me."

"Shut up!" she spat. "Don't say that name again."

"You knew him?" Jaron asked.

She seemed lost, as if sorting through her deepest thoughts and unaware of his presence. "Leviathon's angry with me. How was I to know *he'd* be the one to break the first curse?" she muttered.

25

Jaron's Mother

The key with the Word ... bonded in pressure ... unlock the secret, he read, squatting against the concrete. Even sitting, he could reach out and touch the top and sides of the cage. It was no more than a single arm-span across. The guards had hurled him inside his miniscule prison at Solange's command, slamming the door shut. He drew comfort from the light that filtered in through the air holes, allowing him to read.

Ansel's knife was still tucked in his boot—the guards hadn't searched him. As a Cadet he'd learned the brisk tactic of patting a prisoner down for weapons. Strangely, Solange's guards had overlooked that rudimentary task.

"Why did you have to die?" he questioned in vain, wishing his one true friend was still alive and could explain the mysteries of the *Ancient Way*.

"Talking to yourself, are you?" Solange asked as she entered the room. "I could have taken that book from you when you arrived. Don't think you distracted me with *his* name."

Her grey skin drooped beneath bloodshot eyes and her jaw sagged down, brushing the ruffled collar of her purple gown. Around her head glittered a circle of stones with a solitary blood-red ruby dripping onto her forehead. "Don't worry," she threatened. "I'll take the book and everything else I want soon enough."

Jaron pulled the book to his chest. No matter where he went, *someone* was always trying to snatch his meagre belongings away from him. Perhaps his mother had been wise after all, hiding him in the Heaps—a place where no one valued anything above a morsel of food to survive another day.

"It's time for the blood ritual!" Solange waved at the guard to release Jaron from his pen.

He stumbled out on wobbly legs, cramped from hours of confinement.

"Let's go," she barked.

They wound through a maze of circular passages and Jaron tried to memorize their route, but he soon realized the hopelessness of planning an escape. Even if he seized an opportunity to make a run for it, he'd be twisting blindly, never finding his way back to the underground tunnel.

The path circled higher and narrow slits appeared in the walls. They were above ground now, he assumed. Craning his neck to catch a glimpse of the moon, he pitched forward when the guard jabbed at him to continue up the spiral staircase.

Heat blasted Jaron's lungs as he entered an open space illuminated by the garish glow of hundreds of ochre candles. Lord Drake paced in the centre of the room, swinging a hook-shaped dagger. "Is this the victim?" he growled, breathing heavily.

"No!" Solange directed. "Sit down and wait!"

The shuffle of footsteps echoed up from the staircase. "They're on their way now," she announced needlessly.

Jaron gasped as a girl stumbled into the room followed by another guard. Her golden curls glowed in the candlelight and he recognized the rounded face even without the child-like giggle.

Joelle, his sister.

How could I have mistaken Solange for her? he thought, contrasting Joelle's youth with the haggard stance of the High Priestess.

It seemed that Lord Drake had noticed the mounting transformation in Solange as well. "You're looking overwrought, Priestess. Could it be that your power is waning? Has the great Leviathon abandoned you for someone younger, more deserving?"

"Shut up, you foul-smelling puppet," she said. "The only power you have in the Realm is what I give you. Remember that!" She turned to the guard, asking. "Where's the other one—the one nearer her Birthing Day?"

The guard shifted his weight. "This one says she's pregnant," he answered.

"You fool! I want the other one too! I need her anger at him to provoke his reven—"

She stopped.

"Jaron," she said, a hardened edge to her voice. "This is our sacrifice ... your mother!"

She's insane! he thought. Solange expected him to believe that this girl was his mother. Hadn't the High Priestess guessed who Joelle really was?

"So now you have a choice," Solange purred. "The key, or your mother's life."

"Jaron ... from the Heaps," he heard Joelle whisper as if she remembered him too.

"You can have the key, of course," he answered, discretely winking at Joelle, encouraged that she seemed to know him.

His sister's eyes widened and she cringed.

"Give it to me now!" Solange hissed, her bony arm extended.

Forcing a laugh, he said, "You think I'm stupid enough to bring it with me? Didn't your loyal assistant, Gabria, tell you that I have it safely hidden away?"

"What?" Solange roared, hunching forward as if the weight of her own head was too heavy for her deteriorating spine. "Where is it, you filthy Heapdweller?"

Where is it? he asked himself. What could he invent that would provide even a small glimmer of hope of saving Joelle's life from Solange's blood ritual?

The blaze of the candles choked him, the smothering heat robbing his lungs of oxygen. *The fire,* he remembered, his face now soaked with sweat from the stifling tower air. He'd had the key in his hand before the fire—it had slipped to the ground!

"The farm by the Northern Canal of the Gauntlet," he said with relief. "The one I torched when I went on my Eradication."

He glanced at Joelle, hoping she could tell he was trying to save her life. He wished he could comfort her as her shoulders quivered with silent sobs.

Solange motioned to the guards. "Take him there and don't let him out of your sight," she dictated. "The girl stays with me."

"No!" Jaron yelled. "I won't show them where it is unless I know my … mother … is safe. She comes too, or I won't show anyone where it's hidden." He paused, his thoughts racing to Ansel's knife hidden at his ankle. Could he bring himself to use the knife again to kill someone? *Only for her protection,* he thought, remembering Ansel's letter.

Yet a part of him longed to kill indiscriminately like the other Enforcers. The craving for revenge took root quickly, cultivated by wounded dreams. He discovered he wasn't immune to the desire for self-imposed justice.

"You conniving rat," Solange said. "If you even think I'll send her with you—"

"I won't go with him!" the girl cried out. "Please, just take me back to the Maternity Program. I was wrong to leave. I know that now."

"I will oversee taking her back to the medical facility," Lord Drake said, stepping forward. His eyes devoured the girl as if physically touching her.

Anger seized Jaron as the girl he thought to be his sister crumpled to the ground. "Stay away from her!" he spat.

"There, there, Jaron," Solange crooned, calm briefly masking her growing ugliness. "I've changed my mind. She will go with you as you request." She flung her arm at Lord Drake. "Take the guards. Keep a close watch on her."

"With pleasure," Lord Drake murmured, yanking the girl from the floor.

"Keep your hands off her!" Jaron threw the book to the floor and shoved Lord Drake against the wall.

"Get him!" Lord Drake growled at the guards.

"Wait!" Authority still charged Solange's voice. "Leave him for now. Remember, we still need him to release the key to us." Her bones creaked and groaned as she stooped to collect the book abandoned on the floor. "Thank you for the reminder, Jaron. I'll keep this with me."

His shoulders slumped. He shouldn't have dropped the book. Maybe she would have forgotten …

"Poor boy," Solange said. "It's not your fault. I never intended to let you walk out of here with it. I simply let you read it for awhile to see if you understood any of the passages. Many of the laws governing Leviathon are still a mystery to the Underworld."

She sounded envious, as if Jaron might know something she didn't. Without thinking, a phrase he'd read only moments ago sprung from his lips. "The key and the Word bonded …"

Solange grinned. "You understand as much as I do now. One is useless without the other." She clasped it to her face as if breathing in the scent of the ancient leather would restore her beauty. "Leviathon will reward me for this victory," she crooned. "Now go and bring me the key!"

Lord Drake led the way as the guards marshalled the two prisoners down the stairs and shoved them into the back of a waiting truck.

There was no chance of escape with the doors securely padlocked. Regardless of the hopelessness of the situation, Jaron inhaled deeply, grateful for the chance to be alone with Joelle. "I'm glad Lord Drake is riding up front."

"Stay away from me!" Joelle's face twisted with rage under the glare of the single bulb shining down on them.

"I'm sorry I couldn't stop Solange from finding you," he offered. His sister must hate him for how he'd failed to save her. "But don't worry. I'll think of something to help you get free."

"I don't care about me! You killed my parents! You killed Mama and Papa!" she hurled.

He stared. What did she remember from their life long ago? "I don't know what happened to them ... I was just a Five-Year when Mama left me on a truck bound for the Heaps." *How fitting*, he thought. Life had brought him full circle. Here he was, on another truck bound for the unknown—first to the Heaps, then to the barracks, then to Layden's farm, and now ... to where?

"I heard what you said to that awful woman. *You* burned down the farmhouse. Mama and Papa are *dead*." She clenched her fists. "You're a murderer!"

What was she saying? He mourned how deeply the web of Leviathon wove through the fabric of his life. There had to be some mistake. His mother and father would not have left him, abandoned him, and raised his sister in the warmth of the farmhouse all these years. He'd seen Layden and his wife—no spark of recognition had ignited in his heart. Had Joelle been hidden there, with strangers?

"No, Joelle," he pleaded, trying her name out loud for the first time, hoping she'd believe that they'd once shared happy moments.

"My name is not Joelle! It's Freesia, and I already know everything about *you* from Devora. She told me what you did to her." Her hands were shaking now.

Why did she say her name was Freesia? He refused to believe it. Instead, he grasped for something familiar. "You know Devora? How … where did … where is she? Tell me!"

"Somewhere safe. With Benjamin. He brought me to the castle but left her behind at my parents' farm."

"With Benjamin?" Jaron groaned, his pulse pounding in his ears. "He'll hurt her again."

"You're the one who hurt that girl. She told me the truth. Right now she's taking shelter in my family's barn. It's the only thing left after you burned our home to the ground and shot my parents in cold blood."

The truck swerved and she flew forward, bouncing against Jaron. He reached out to steady her but she recoiled as if he were a monster.

"It's not your parents' farm," he mumbled, still trying to sort through the tangle of deceit. "You're Joelle, my sister. Don't you remember? Our Papa died a long time ago in his search for the Crimson River."

"You're mad!"

Snatching the note from his trouser pocket and dropping it in her lap, he said. "Look. This was in the book Solange took from me."

"And you're a thief too," she said, tears welling up in her eyes. "That book belonged to my father. The one *you* killed."

He clenched his teeth. "I … I know I did a horrible thing when I followed the order to burn the farmhouse, but Layden forgave me. Whether you believe me or not, I didn't kill them."

"You wrote this note!" she accused. "It's a fraud. Like you!"

"No!" Jaron said, convinced she wouldn't believe him no matter what he said. "It was already inside the book when I rescued it from the house. I tried to return the book to Layden but he asked me to keep it ... and find you ... his daughter." As he spoke the words, he realized she couldn't be Joelle. Emptiness filled him, a strange sensation of hollowness expanding until there was no room left for even the tiniest sliver of hope.

"You're lying. Mama and Papa kept that book under glass. They said it was sacred, not to be touched. They wouldn't give it to you." She struck wildly at his chest.

A man's voice cut through the stale air, and before Jaron could think to pause the voice recorder in his shirt pocket, Layden's words echoed, absolving Jaron of wrongdoing.

Freesia shrank back, pain etching her face as she came to terms with the bitter truth.

"I'm sorry that you had to hear his final 'goodbye' this way," he said, mercifully pressing the stop button before the shots rang out. It would have been better to let her think that he was guilty than to cause her any more pain.

"Papa's voice ... those were his last words ..." she looked down, trying to compose herself so she could speak, "... thank you." Then she closed her eyes and sighed. "And I believe you. You seem more ... balanced than Benjamin. You can't have been the one who hurt Devora. But that still doesn't change that I'm not your sister."

"I know," he said as the truck braked again and she tumbled forward. This time when he reached out to help her, she didn't pull away.

26
Evil Unmasked

Devora awoke to the sweet scent of clean straw and a slight rustling noise. A shadow blocked the pale light cast from the oil lamp—Benjamin was watching her.

Startled, she tugged her blanket around her and then sighed deeply. Although his hair was cropped close to his scalp, his brown eyes were … human, as they used to be months ago in the Heaps before Jaron had stolen Benjamin's shelter, before . . . everything.

"How long have I been sleeping?" she asked, rising to her feet. Her body, torn and bruised from childbirth, protested the movement.

"A few hours, I guess," he answered. "I took Freesia to Lord Drake's castle, but then I came back to you as soon as I could."

"Why'd you take *her* there?"

"Captain Mar ordered it because she's Jaron's mother."

"What?" Devora gasped, shaking her head to clear the lingering cobwebs of sleep. "Benjamin! She's the same age as we are!"

"So?"

"There's no way she could be his mother."

"If you say so." He shrugged, kicking at a bale of hay. "They wanted me to bring you too," he said. "But I saw you lying there asleep. You looked … peaceful."

His eyes had lost their wild appearance as the three of them had trekked back toward the farm. Benjamin had cut through the forest, covering the distance in days rather than the weeks it had taken them to follow the river north. Even so, he'd run out of the white pills he'd gulped on the first day and the effects now seemed to be gone.

"Why didn't you take me to the castle?" she cried, daring to strike him in the chest. "Freesia's always the one who gets the special treatment!"

"You don't get it, Devora," he said, restraining her arms to prevent her feeble attempts to hit him again.

She slumped back, pulling away from him. "What are you talking about?"

Cracking his knuckles one-by-one, he said. "Jaron's still a Cadet. He needs to pass a test."

"And what does that have to do with Freesia parading around Lord Drake's castle being waited on hand and foot all over again?" she asked, envisioning Freesia lounging in the atrium of the White Palace sipping fruit juice and munching on teacakes.

"A Cadet becomes an Enforcer when he eradicates, or *kills*, his mother," Benjamin said in a whisper. "Even if Freesia's not Jaron's mother, I think they'll tell him she is."

"Oh," Devora winced. Benjamin's attentiveness toward her had increased during their journey, gradually thawing the ice encasing her heart. Now that she was here with him, finally secure, she allowed herself to glimpse beyond her own need.

"I kept you here in the barn, hoping it would save your life." He reached for her and she fell against him.

"You rescued me," she whispered, tears sliding off her cheeks and onto his shirt. "But why didn't you help me that night in the Heaps?"

"When?" he asked, gripping her more tightly.

Cocooned in his embrace, she searched for the words to describe the brutal act Jaron had committed. She sketched the barest of details, including just enough for Benjamin to comprehend how she'd been violated.

He shoved her away and began to pace, stomping around in the stale straw. "So that thing, that *baby*, at the waterfall belonged to *you*? And you left it there!" he yelled. "You're no better than a Holding Shell!"

Wrapping her arms around her thin shoulders, she shivered. "You made me leave it!" she cried and guilt crowded in on her. She'd said nothing. Freesia had been the only one to plead that the baby be saved. "Besides, it's Jaron's fault. He hurt me!" She clawed at the damp straw, desperate for Benjamin's approval despite her growing self-loathing.

"You're right, it is," Benjamin replied mechanically, swinging his fists through the air. "I'll take care of him too. I'm not an Enforcer for nothing!"

She stared at him as the curtain of safety that had draped around her earlier was snatched away. "You're not a Cadet anymore, like Jaron?"

His eyes revealed to her that he grasped the significance of the question. "No!" he shouted, storming out of the barn.

He's killed his mother.

Crouching forward, she cradled her empty abdomen. *Is this all there is to my life—being alone ... an empty shell?*

Hearing a vehicle, she crept toward the door and the headlights blinded her momentarily. *Benjamin, where are you? I don't want to be alone, no matter what you've done.*

Metal doors slammed shut. "Get the prisoners!" a fat, hairy man ordered.

Guards pushed two people out of the shadows.

"Freesia!" Devora cried, seeing the familiar face. She ran to her, throwing her arms around the other girl's neck. "I thought Jaron killed you!"

"No," Freesia whispered. "You have to listen, Devora. I don't believe Jaron is the one who hurt you. He's . . . trying to save me."

"What!" Devora said, glaring past Freesia as the second prisoner strode in front of the unforgiving lights shining from the truck. "Jaron!"

"It wasn't me, Devora." He kept his face expressionless, as if awaiting her judgment.

She trembled, heat surging through her veins. "Liar!" she shrieked. "Rat-faced liar! I'll kill you with my bare hands."

"Wait!" Freesia begged. "First, just listen to what he has to say."

"I'm done listening."

"Move out of the way, Devora," Benjamin growled, appearing from the shadows and shoving her aside. "I'll take care of Jaron before he says another word."

Devora's heart raced. She didn't need Benjamin to fight this battle for her. She didn't want anyone's help anymore. "Get out of my way!" she said, prepared to sacrifice her own worthless self to release her rage.

The guards restrained Devora as the fat man massaged his hands together. "This works even better," he gloated. "Fight to the death, Jaron! Strike a blow in revenge for Devora's attack. Then the key will be mine."

Benjamin charged forward, his shoulder ploughing into Jaron's gut. "Get up and fight me, you coward!"

Devora collapsed, her adrenalin spent.

"Let me help you to your feet," the fat man offered, extending his hand to her.

The unmistakable odour of cold desire permeated the air, threatening to snuff out her very being. Devora recoiled in horror. "It was *you*," she said, knowing, remembering the stench of sweat and vile hunger that had overpowered her that night. "Who are you?" she said, as if knowing his name gave her some power over what he'd robbed from her.

"Stupid Heapdwellers!" he scoffed. "You should know who *I* am by now. I am Lord Drake, your Leader."

She broke away from her attacker as Benjamin pummelled Jaron's face with a blow that made his nose spurt blood. "Stop!" she begged, running out between them. "Stop it now, both of you. It wasn't Jaron who hurt me."

Benjamin pulled back his fist, eyeing her suspiciously. "You're feeling sorry for him now?"

"No. It wasn't him!"

Benjamin backed away, his breathing erratic.

Jaron ripped off his shirt and bunched it up to stop the blood gushing from his nose. "You know the truth?" Jaron asked her, his voice muffled.

"Yes," she said, reaching to touch his shoulder. "I'm so sorry you were hurt."

"There's something you need to hear, Devora," he said, his chest heaving from exertion. "I'll fight for your protection every day for the rest of my life, but I can't . . . I won't kill out of revenge. It's too important. To the future—to *our* future."

"I don't care," she said, wrapping her arms around him.

"How delightful," Lord Drake snarled, his guards flanking his sides. "Seize her!"

"No!" Jaron positioned himself in front of her. "You'll have to kill me first."

"And me." Benjamin joined Jaron, the two of them forming an unstoppable wall face to face with the guards.

"Draw your guns!" Lord Drake shouted. "Hurry, you useless fools!"

His orders came too late. With one decisive snap, Jaron broke the arm of one guard while Benjamin pinned the other to the ground, crushing his groin.

Coolly, Lord Drake gave Benjamin an appraising look. "I see you have an attachment to this piece of trash. Your allegiance to the Realm is most certainly in question, but I can understand the enticing pull of a woman, no matter how worthless she might be. She's yours."

"Benjamin," Jaron said, pulling away from Devora slightly and unsheathing the knife from its hiding place in his boot. "Stay away from her, do you hear me? We're leaving this place as soon as I find my key, and if you try to hurt her again, like you did that night in the Heaps, I'll do what I must to protect her."

Devora couldn't believe Jaron's words. Solange had twisted everything! Both of them, Jaron and Benjamin, had thought the other guilty of her attack. "No, Benjamin, don't leave," she said, dropping her hand on his arm. "I know it wasn't you either."

"What?" Jaron said. "But I saw him by your shelter that night."

"And I saw you," Benjamin accused.

"Well if it wasn't either of them, who was it?" Freesia asked.

"Him," Devora said, pointing to the fat man.

"I'll kill him!" Benjamin hollered, barrelling toward the Leader of the Realm. He locked his arm around Lord Drake's neck.

"No, Benjamin! Don't! Lord Drake's not worth it," Jaron cried out.

Benjamin whirled around, his eyes sober. "It's all I'm good for." With the two guards writhing in pain, Lord Drake stood alone—vulnerable. Benjamin shoved the abandoned leader toward the barn.

"Stop him! I order you!" Lord Drake whined to his defeated guards. Helpless, he stayed securely in Benjamin's grip, a crumpled shell of his former self.

"After I'm done with this mound of garbage," Benjamin threatened the guards, "I'll be back for both of you."

Leaning on one another, the guards turned their backs. The one with the broken arm hoisted himself into the driver's seat and revved the engine, drowning out the fading screams of their fallible leader as they raced away.

"Now what do we do?" Devora whispered.

Freesia slipped out of the shadows and enveloped Devora in a warm hug. "We'll go back to the waterfall and find Riak … and your baby."

"Oh," Devora cried out, "I left her all alone!" Her insides twisted until she felt as though she'd swallowed barbed wire. Benjamin was right—she was no better than a Holding Shell.

"Shh," Freesia comforted. "I'm sure Riak came back and found her. He knows how to look after babies."

"I hope so," Devora whimpered. "But he said she was too small. Born too early."

Freesia nodded. "She was. But I've read that some premature babies survive with … I don't know. Hey, where did Jaron go?"

A pang of jealousy stabbed through Devora as she heard the affection in Freesia's voice. First Riak, and now Jaron, catered to this girl as if she were royalty.

27

He Knows My Name

"Is there a place we can hide until daylight?" Jaron asked, returning a few minutes later.

"What about the barn?" Devora suggested.

He shook his head. "Solange knows where we are. Even though I doubt the guards will be in a hurry to report their failure, it's not safe to stay."

"Riak's family lives nearby," Freesia offered reluctantly. "His father might give us supplies for the journey." Doubt nagged at her. How could she ask him for more when Riak was missing?

"We should go, then," Jaron said.

Walking in the darkness, Freesia recalled the carefree days when she had travelled this way to visit her childhood companion, unaware of what Leviathon was really like. It shamed her to think it, but she resented the knowledge she'd acquired in recent weeks. She would turn back the clock in an instant if it were possible. All the years she'd valued the "truth" of her lessons mocked her as she longed to live in ignorance once again.

"How much further?" Devora finally asked.

Freesia stopped. She'd been wondering that herself. They should have arrived at the other farm by now. "It's not usually so far ... I'm sorry ... I think I've lost my way in the dark."

"We should stop, then," Jaron said. "We'll find our way back in the morning."

"Back where?" Devora asked, her voice tense. "Aren't we going to the waterfall right away to find my ... to find Riak?"

"I can't leave without at least *trying* to find my key."

"That key!" Devora spat. "It's caused you more harm than good. Did you ever think it might be cursed?"

Jaron inhaled sharply, as if he'd been struck.

Recalling how he'd defended her in the tower, Freesia felt like she had a debt to repay. "I need to see my parents' grave. To say goodbye. I may never be back this way again."

"Fine!" Devora snapped. "I guess *you two* have already made up your minds."

The night chill crept into Freesia's bones and she didn't rest well on the forest floor. For the first time she wondered about the identity of her own baby's father. It didn't seem to matter over three new moons ago when she'd arrived at the medical facility. At that point, her anticipation of being admitted to such a prestigious program had overshadowed any questions and unspoken fears—Leviathon had extended an invitation to serve and she had blindly complied.

By dawn, her body ached for a peaceful sleep that had never materialized.

"We should move quickly," Jaron said.

Freesia admired his face: determined, yet kind. When he'd first suggested they were siblings in the back of that truck she'd been sickened by what she thought he was. Now she longed to have family again. To belong.

Soon I'll have a child as my family. The thought frightened her. She wasn't prepared to tackle this alone. Experts were supposed to be raising her baby so that she'd be free to live her own life— she had hoped it would be a life with Riak.

The charred ruins of her home came into view and raw dread filled her heart. *But their bodies won't be there this time*, she reminded herself, hoping she could find her parents' graves quickly.

Her wish was granted. In the distance, under a shady willow, were two fresh mounds of dirt surrounded by stones. "Oh ..." she said as tears sprang to her eyes.

"Someone else was buried here quite some time ago," Jaron whispered, pointing to a grassy mound also marked by stones. He and Freesia stood side-by-side as Devora waited in the distance. He'd first scouted the area, taking his time before deciding it was safe to approach the graveside. So far, the Enforcers hadn't appeared.

"I had a twin brother who must have died when I was very young. His name was Aaron," Freesia said. "Mama and Papa would never speak of him. This could be his grave."

Jaron's memory flashed like a bullet hitting its target.

"Happy birthday, Joelle."

"Happy birthday, Aaron," his twin Joelle said, her blue eyes sparkling.

"No, silly Joelle, that's not right! Watch how I say it, J-J-Jaron."

"J-J ... Aaron," Joelle repeated, scooping up a fistful of cake.

"That's what my sister called me—Aaron," he said, his heart quickening with rising hope as he tried to untwist another layer of truth. "Joelle never could say my name properly. She called me Aaron. I'd forgotten we were twins."

"Oh!" Freesia stammered, clamping her hands over her mouth. She stared past him as if locked in a dream of her own. "I was with Papa, watching him as he shovelled dirt into a fresh mound just like these. There was a man ... lying in a hole. I touched the man's face and Papa yelled at me to move away."

She stopped, focusing on Jaron. "The man's face was like ice."

"Do you remember anything else about that day?" he prompted.

She closed her eyes. "Sweat dripped from his nose as he carved the trench. I kept saying over and over, 'Papa, Papa, what's wrong?'" She buried her face in her hands. "Oh! Oohh! Papa, please forgive me!" she sobbed.

"What?" Jaron asked. He felt as though time stood still.

She wiped away her tears with her sleeve and stared straight at Jaron. "I'd forgotten until now that the man I was calling Papa was the one lying cold on the ground."

"Joelle," he whispered, unable to say anything else. Finally he'd found her, his sister—his family. He wrapped his arms around her, pulling her close, and the years they'd been separated no longer mattered.

"We should look for the key now," she said, wiping her eyes again. "Enough has been taken from us already."

"I dropped it in the dirt when I started the fire," Jaron admitted quietly. He hated saying the words out loud to his newly found sister. "I wish I had disobeyed that order."

"It wouldn't have mattered," Freesia said. "You said yourself that Captain Mar would have shot you and lit the fire himself if you'd refused."

Jaron knew she spoke the truth, but that didn't lift the guilt that weighted his thoughts. He was a coward. What was his life worth that he should live and others should die? The two of them began sifting through the dirt and ashes, trying to find something of value.

"It's like you're back in the Heaps, isn't it Jaron?" Devora scowled, approaching them. "Digging through the dirt, searching for treasure. Except you two seem pretty cosy about it."

"There's something wonderful you should know about Jaron and me," Freesia said as she stood up next to Devora.

"What?" Devora's mouth pinched tight again.

"He's my brother."

Jaron listened to the pride in Freesia's voice and hoped he would one day live up to the faith she seemed to have in him.

"Oh … oh … OH!" Devora sputtered.

"I know," Freesia said. "Jaron says my name used to be Joelle, but I want to be called Freesia in memory of them." She nodded toward the graves. "They were good parents."

The sun climbed higher over the trees and sweat beaded on Jaron's soot-smeared face. He knew they shouldn't stay much longer although he wished things could be different—even Layden's paint-chipped barn would be a palace compared to his hovel in the Heaps. "I think we should forget the key and go," he forced himself to say. After all, he wasn't alone anymore; he'd found his family—Freesia and Devora—and he needed to protect them.

"We can't!" Freesia said, digging more frantically. "This key is now a part of who I am too. And what if someone else finds it and gives it to Solange?"

He nodded. "Then I'll see if there's a rake or a tool in the barn. That might help speed things up."

Inside, he found Layden's collection of simple tools. He selected a rake and a sieve, hoping they'd make finding the key easier. A noise made him spin around.

"Don't come any closer," Benjamin said. A streak of dried blood marked his face.

"Where have you been? Where's Lord Drake?" Jaron asked.

"Someplace where he won't ever hurt anyone again," Benjamin answered, wiping his cheek with his wet sleeve, diluting the bloodstain to a rosy pink.

Jaron stared at his long ago friend, grieving the loss as if Benjamin himself had died. Leviathon had stolen the best part of all its citizens, and still—some losses seemed more painful than others. "What will you do?"

Now clear-eyed and solemn, Benjamin shrugged.

"Come with us."

Benjamin smiled, his eyes heavy, vacant, yet absent of their former thirst for carnage. "Do you trust me?"

"I don't know … it's a difficult thing, Benjamin, I—"

The Enforcer stepped forward. "Don't say any more. How can you trust me when I don't trust myself?" He brushed past Jaron. "Tell Devora I said goodbye," he said, slipping away through a back door.

Inhaling deeply, Jaron straightened his shoulders and carried the tools outside. "Benjamin was in the barn and said to tell you goodbye."

"Where is he?" Devora asked.

"Gone," Jaron said simply.

"You didn't stop him?" Devora accused.

"He's a killer, Devora. He's not the friend we once knew."

"I don't believe that," she said, returning to her digging. "He protected me."

They toiled together, Jaron kneading the ground with the rake and the girls scooping handfuls of debris into the sieve.

"I found it!" Jaron whispered moments later when his fingers embraced the familiar shape. He knew every detail by heart—it was a part of him. Tying a new knot in the cord, he slipped the key over his neck saying, "We must go."

"But what about Benjamin?" Devora asked.

"He's a part of our past," Jaron said, looking toward the three graves. "Like the dead buried here, we have to leave our past behind."

She nodded.

Gathering some stale oats and dried corn from the barn, the three of them followed the river northward, walking in silence.

Although he was relieved to have found his key, Jaron struggled with the reminder of the Ancient Way and Ansel's death. By afternoon it began to rain, pelting down icy drops until his shoulders were numb from the cold.

"It's no use," Devora said, collapsing by the raging water. "By now Solange must know we've escaped." She shuddered, wiping her dripping nose with her sleeve. "You don't know her like I do. She can find us anywhere with her magic."

"Or the Enforcers and their dogs will track us down," Freesia added. "Even Benjamin found us the last time. He knew a shortcut from the waterfall to the castle."

"Oh!" Devora said. "Solange doesn't even need the dogs! She used to appear from nowhere."

"You didn't see her yesterday, Devora. Her magic is growing weaker, I think," Jaron said, remembering the drooping features of the High Priestess.

"Why?" Freesia asked.

He shrugged. "I'm not sure. I think she gets her power from Leviathon and something's changed. Something to do with my friend Ansel and his death." *There*, he'd finally opened his secret wound for them to glimpse and see who he really was—a killer.

"What are you talking about? A friend? Who is Ansel?" Devora stared suspiciously.

He told them. Everything.

The rain slackened to a light drizzle and the sun pushed its way through the clouds. Heartened by his sister's encouraging smile, Jaron found a dry spot under a broad evergreen for them to rest for a few moments.

"Who would ever believe one could have such a friend?" Devora hugged her knees, suddenly jumping at the sound of a loud crack. "What was that noise?"

"Shh," Jaron whispered. "Quiet! Someone's coming!" He turned his head toward the snapping of wet twigs. The footsteps grew closer. Jaron reached for the knife he had tucked back into his boot. Was Benjamin returning for the final revenge?

"Visitors this far north?" a loud voice boomed. "It's unheard of!"

Jaron blinked. "Who are you?" he asked, staring at the tallest man he'd ever seen.

"A hunter, Son. Just a simple hunter. The name's Zarek." He dropped a heavy pack to the ground and untied the flap. "You folks look like you could use some supplies."

He tossed three cloaks to them. "Put these on before you catch your death."

Zarek collected some dry needles from under the evergreen and added a few damp sticks to start a fire.

"I don't think we should—" Freesia began.

"Nonsense!" the hunter laughed. "There's no one around for miles. No good reason why we shouldn't heat up a little soup to go with our bread."

The warm food worked its way into Jaron's belly, heating him from the inside out. "Thank you," he said, draining the last drop from the tin cup.

"Take some food for the journey ahead," Zarek offered, bundling up more bread and portions of fruit and cheese.

"You've been very kind," Jaron said. "You remind me of a friend I once had."

"All is not as it seems, Jaron," the hunter said, staring down with a hearty smile. "Remember that."

As Zarek slipped away into the forest, Jaron wondered, *How did he know my name?*

28
Dead or Alive?

"She was born too soon. Her lungs were weak," Riak said, reverently holding a cocooned bundle.

Devora lowered her head. "I'm sorry I left her."

"It wouldn't have mattered," Jaron said, awkwardly touching Devora. "Riak said he found her soon after you left, remember? She wasn't alone for long."

After two weeks of wearying travel, Jaron, Devora, and Freesia had come upon the clearing as the mid-morning sun sparkled in the churning pool of water beneath the falls. Riak was there, hobbling on a crude walking stick, still recovering from his fall the night he'd left Freesia and Devora in search of a passageway.

"But no one else could feed her except for me."

"I gave her water and wild honey soaked in a cloth. My father fed that to my sister when my mother was too sick to nurse. You couldn't have done anything more," Riak said. "She fought valiantly until last night. I kept her warm but she needed a doctor."

Her eyes wet, Devora said, "But I could have held her."

"You can hold her now," Riak offered.

By late afternoon Devora allowed herself to sip some water that Jaron gave to her. "I don't know how you can look at me after what I've done," she whispered.

"We're all guilty of something, Devora," he said, leaving her to grieve.

He sat beside Freesia at the river's edge. "I have my key back, but without the book we're sitting here trapped by the mountain," he said, desperate to understand what it all meant. What secrets had Leviathon been searching for? "I'm still no closer to discovering the Ancient Way or finding home."

"What do you remember from what you read?" Freesia asked.

"The Crimson River crosses a mountain."

Riak ran his hand through his hair. "This is the only river. I'm sure of it."

"And it's not crimson," Jaron muttered. This mountain was a dead end. Maybe there was nowhere else, nothing to search for— or worse still, nothing to live for. He shook his head, staring at the top of the mountain. The sun dipped in the sky, casting a brilliant glow of fire before it relinquished the horizon to the moonlight.

"The Crimson River," he whispered, pointing to the fiery rays reflecting on the water. He tore the key from his neck, sprinting toward the wall of rock flanking the waterfall. Maybe there was a secret passage like the one that tunnelled into Solange's hideaway.

"Help me!" he said, probing the rocks.

"What are you looking for?" Freesia asked.

"A lever, something that moves, anything. Just look!" He reached for a smooth stone as if it had called out to him. He tugged and it shifted sideways. The ground rumbled and groaned as the rock opened, revealing a passageway.

"Oh my ..." Freesia gasped.

"Let's go!" Jaron said, running back to get Devora. "We'll bury your baby once we find a home," he promised.

Clutching his key, Jaron led them into the mountain passage. Riak flashed an electric torch to light their way. Devora followed close behind him, whispering to the mute bundle in her arms. They wound through the mountain on level ground. Jaron breathed a sigh of relief that they weren't descending into the murky depths of the earth like when he had journeyed into the castle with Gabria.

It didn't take long for them to reach a door.

"It's locked," Freesia said, fingering the iron deadbolt.

Trembling, Jaron tested his key in the lock.

Nothing.

"The key and the Word bonded," Jaron whispered weakly. "We need the book."

"Let's just go back to the river," Devora said.

Freesia grabbed Riak's hand. "I guess we have no other choice."

They turned back and were exiting the tunnel under a starlit sky when a green glow appeared before them.

"I've found you at last, dear child," Solange hissed.

Devora cowered behind Jaron.

"Tsk, tsk, so disobedient. I lost track of you." The High Priestess shuffled closer with the familiar red book gripped in her pale fingers. Her brilliant glow had vanished, replaced by an eerie pallor covering her sagging cheeks. "After some creative convincing, Benjamin told me where I might find you. You owe me the key, Jaron."

"You're losing your magic," Jaron said, boldly striding toward the High Priestess. "Has the great Leviathon abandoned you like Lord Drake said in the tower? Or is it the great Leviathon himself who has no power?"

As he said the words he remembered his conversation with Ansel. It seemed a lifetime ago. What was it Ansel had said? *The enemy has no power outside the borders of Leviathon.* After spending a few days in the Enforcer program, Jaron had thought the enemy Ansel referred to was Lord Drake. But what if Ansel had really meant something darker—Leviathon himself?

Jaron reached for the book and felt a blast of fire bolt through him.

"I still have enough magic to take care of you," Solange cackled, gripping the book. "If only you'd used that knife in revenge."

His eyes flew open.

"You thought I didn't know about that. Why do you think my guards didn't bother to search you? I wanted you to use it. But now perhaps you'll willingly give me the key when I tell you that I really *do* know where your mother is."

"Don't believe her," Freesia said.

"Give me the key," Solange repeated.

"I will. Inside the mountain," Jaron said, stepping toward the passageway. If he was right, Solange would have no power once she stepped through the entrance, for she would be outside of the boundaries of Leviathon. "Riak, Devora and Freesia, go ahead of me!"

The High Priestess hobbled forward, following them through the opening. "You worthless rat!" she sputtered, comprehending what Jaron had done. "Leviathon, where are you? How can you abandon me after I gave you everything?" she whimpered in a low guttural moan and stumbled back outside.

Dropping to her knees, Solange's skin turned ashen grey—all evidence of her former shimmering glory seeped away. Her final breath was expelled into a pool of her own blood.

"What happened?" Riak's mouth gaped open at the sight of Solange's lifeless body.

"I only thought she'd lose her power. I didn't know ..."

As he stared at the aged shell of a woman, Jaron felt one of Devora's arms slide around his middle. "We're safe," she said, sighing. "Lord Drake is gone. Solange is gone." She glanced down at the tiny bundle cradled against her. "I can find a resting place for this little one."

"It's over," Freesia agreed. "Riak can go back to his family now."

"We'll all go back." Riak took Freesia's hand. "My parents have enough room for everyone. We'll have a home."

Home. The journey was over.

Jaron reached for the key, now back around his neck where it had been kept safe for so many years. "I don't know," he whispered, pulling the cord tight. "What if there's more to the promise? What if this passage leads us to better place?"

"The Realm of Leviathon is safe now. It can be our home." Devora's eyes held a promising flicker of hope.

"Check Papa's book, Jaron. It will tell us. I'm sure of it."

The book had fallen behind Solange's body, just outside the entrance of the passageway. Jaron reached for it and a shimmering foot planted itself firmly on his hand. "Nice try," Gabria hissed.

Jaron stared up at his former nurse. *Had she always been so ... beautiful?* "You look different," he sputtered.

Devora tugged on his arm. "Be careful, Jaron, she glows ... like Solange."

Gabria's head snapped back, her dark curls bouncing as radiant amber lights reflected from her silken hair. "I'm nothing like Solange," she coaxed, reaching for Jaron's hand. "She was weak and stupid, blind to those around her who were waiting to stab her in the back. I stayed focused on the will of Leviathon and now here I am, the reigning High Priestess."

"You're no High Priestess!" Jaron spat out. "You're a Heapdweller just like me."

She smiled. "I know exactly who and what I am. I've worked too hard to get here to be distracted by your petty insults. I was the top Interrogator in the Realm, remember? I lied to you. You remind me of no one." She held out her hand. "Now, give me the key or my guards will dispose of your little group of friends. *They* can still overpower you inside the passageway."

"Don't do it!" Devora pleaded.

Gabria eyed the bundle in Devora's arms. "What's that?"

"Leave her alone," Devora said drawing the bundle close.

"It's dead, isn't it? Convince Jaron to give me the key and I'll bring the child back to life."

"Don't listen to her, Devora," Freesia urged. "She's a liar."

Jaron watched Devora grip the baby as silent tears slid off her cheeks onto the blanket. He understood her need for redemption—it mirrored his own.

"We're going to find a way through this mountain even without the book," Jaron said, nodding his head toward a lever inside the secret entrance. Would Devora understand? If only they could shut it and jam the mechanism before Gabria found the stone lever on the outside …

"Give me the key, Jaron," Devora said, trembling as she gripped the bundle.

"No, Devora, you can't trust that woman," Freesia warned.

"It'll be okay, I promise. Even if you don't trust her, you can trust me, right Jaron?" she asked. Her face was expressionless as she blinked twice and glanced at the lever.

"I trust you," he said, understanding the secret code they had used to communicate in the Heaps.

Slinging the key around her neck, Devora stepped across the threshold into the light of Gabria's glow. "Now!" she screamed, shoving the bundle at the new High Priestess and snatching the red book from her hands. Devora dove back through the opening as the stone slammed shut.

"Find something to bar the door!" Jaron shouted, his eyes on the door, hoping Gabria wouldn't be able to open it before they could jam it securely into place.

"Here," Riak said, tossing the walking stick he'd been using to Jaron.

Bracing the door with the stick, Jaron could hear Gabria's torrent of insults and curses fading away. The High Priestess eventually gave up, but not without shouting one final taunt. "I have your baby, Devora. My magic will revive her."

Devora's face paled as she gripped the book.

"She's lying to you," Freesia whispered. "Her magic's not *that* strong."

"Let's go back through the tunnel," Jaron urged, placing his arm around Devora's thin shoulders. "We'll try the door once more."

Tufts of moss cascaded down the damp walls of the passageway. Listening to the steady thud of footfalls against the packed clay, Jaron wondered who had carved this way of escape. Or was it a way of death? Were they destined to live out their remaining days caught like rats in a trap?

For the second time, Jaron stood helpless before the ancient door. Not a glimmer of light spilled through the keyhole as, again, his attempt to twist his key in the lock failed.

Devora waved the book at him. "There has to be something in here or they all wouldn't have wanted it so badly!"

Staring at the outline of the key on the cover, Jaron muttered, "The key with the Word bonded."

"What are you saying?" Freesia asked.

"Pass it here, Devora." Jaron placed his key on top of the image and the two sacred pieces snapped together.

"It's a magnet!" Riak gasped.

"Now what?" Freesia asked.

"In pressure, it unlocks the secret," Jaron whispered, depressing the key into the inlay. The cover slid open, revealing an engraved inscription inside.

> *Call out to the one who hears the cry of the desolate,*
> *The friend who laid down his life.*
> *All is not as it seems.*

"The words of Zarek, the hunter," Jaron said. "*The friend*—it must mean Ansel. But how can it be, when he's dead?"

Riak spoke. "From what you all have said, there's more to this Ancient Way than any of us are able to understand. Gabria and Solange had their magic to make the impossible possible. Maybe this Ansel has some power you don't know about."

The book felt like live coals in Jaron's hand and his heart raced in hope at Riak's words. "I don't know what to do," he admitted.

"We're at the door and that key didn't work," Freesia said. "It's time to try something else."

Jaron turned away from them. "Help?" he said feebly, feeling stupid that he was talking to the door. "Help me, Ansel," he called out, his voice louder.

Nothing happened.

"Try it again," Devora urged.

"Ansel! If you can hear me, we are in trouble and we need your help!" Jaron shouted.

The ground trembled as if awaking from a deep slumber, sending bits of mud and loose stones cascading down around them. Jaron pulled Devora close and covered her head with his own. With his lips pressed against her hair, he awaited the tunnel's collapse. He felt no fear, simply disappointment. Death lurked behind every door in the Realm of Leviathon. Jaron was surprised they had managed to cheat fate until now. Against the odds, they had made it out of the Garbage Heaps and beyond the boundaries of Leviathon, but he resolved that they had reached the end.

Suddenly, a quiet stillness and an awakening light flooded the passageway.

"This is as far as you can travel without me," Ansel said. He stood before them, radiating a light more intensely pure and powerful than the pale counterfeit glow of Gabria or Solange.

Jaron, sure he was now dreaming, fell back against the wall of the passage to steady himself. "But you're dead!"

"I couldn't tell you everything before," Ansel said, raising his hand to display a golden key. "I had to die in order to take this back from the grip of Leviathon. He's trapped in the Underworld and uses mortals to kill and destroy for his amusement. It took three days of fighting *him*, but I won." The key shimmered, its design in the shape of a crossroads.

"Three days? You died new moons ago," Jaron whispered. "Why did you wait until now to appear? I needed you."

"I answered when you called."

Jaron stared at the dull metal key still locked in the cover of the book.

"Your key was a symbol of the promise, beckoning you to search for home," Ansel said, as if answering Jaron's silent question. Turning to include the rest of them, he added, "What I have done for Jaron, I have done for you all. I am the door to home, follow me."

"Wait!" Riak shouted as the others moved to follow. "My father—my family, I can't leave them behind. They won't know anything about this home."

Jaron wavered. Riak was right. His father was gone, but what if his mother *was* still alive? And what about Benjamin? Had he slipped away forever into Leviathon's grasp?

"You all know the secret now," Ansel said. Once you step through the doorway, I'll help you build a shelter, a home. I'll teach you to fight the remaining magic of Leviathon and then you can go back and help your families. Each of you must decide for yourself, but you are all welcome."

Ansel touched the door that had blocked their path only moments before and it vanished, revealing the warmth of daylight on the other side. Fields of wildflowers nodded a peaceful welcome as, one by one, they stepped over the threshold.

They were *home*.

Epilogue

"You've chosen well." Ansel smiled.

"I've learned that I need reminders to follow the path of the Ancient Way." Jaron fingered the key again strung around his neck. "Without this in the Heaps, I might have given up, forgotten to search for truth."

"Possibly," Ansel said. "But I think your heart would always have sought for home."

Jaron pondered Ansel's words. His friend seemed to peer into the hidden motives of their hearts, but Jaron wondered if he really knew their deepest failings.

"The path isn't always clear," Ansel said, warmly clasping Jaron's shoulder. "But here you are, with your shelter in the Fields of Savai."

Smiling, Jaron inhaled the fragrant wildflowers. Only weeks after their first view of home, Ansel had encouraged them all to begin building. Jaron knew immediately that he wanted to live close to the mountain—near the passageway that had led them home.

The others joined them to eat and Ansel spread out a meal of fragrant spiced meat and vegetables. "Enjoy," he said. "You'll need your strength for the days ahead."

"When does our training start?" Riak asked, passing a bowl of luscious fruit to Freesia.

Jaron tried not to envy the affection Riak and Freesia had for one another. After all, it was right that she had someone to watch over her like he did with Devora. Soon his sister would have her Birthing Day.

"Your training has already begun," Ansel replied.

Jaron grinned. Their friend and mentor hadn't changed. His words were still measured, sometimes a mystery, allowing them to make their own choices and possibly even their own mistakes.

"You said that one day we could go back through the mountain," Devora said, her brow furrowed. "When can we do that?"

"In time," Ansel replied. "When you understand how to fight your enemy."

She played with the food on her plate. Jaron wished she would smile more. It seemed as if she was physically with them but her heart was lost somewhere else. He grieved that he hadn't been able to keep his promise to bury her infant near her new home. The child's body had been traded for the book—another sacrifice of the innocent.

"Please tell us more about the Underground," Riak asked. "You mentioned them the last time we ate together."

Ansel's eyes focused on a distant mountain peak. "They are fellow Keepers of the Key and other believers in the Ancient Way. They've been forced into hiding and are falsely accused of violent acts that are, in fact, perpetrated by the Enforcers."

An element of understanding flashed through Jaron. "The bridge explosion and the fire at the farm," he said. "Both were to be blamed on someone else. Was it the Underground?"

Nodding, Ansel said, "The Enforcers commit crimes and accuse the Underground in an effort to discredit them … and to discredit the Ancient Way."

"We need to help them," Riak said.

"You will," Ansel said.

"In time?" Riak grinned.

"Yes. In time."

Devora sliced the loaf of freshly baked bread and shared a piece with the others as Ansel talked. *Jaron looks so content,* she thought. *Why can't I be happy?*

Finally, the others drifted away, and she and Jaron sat alone as the sun dropped low.

"Ansel said the baby is safe in the Great Beyond, Devora. You have to trust him," Jaron said as if reading her brooding thoughts.

It was a topic they'd sparred over before. "Ansel also said Leviathon rules the Underworld. What if my baby's there in that evil place?"

"Ansel doesn't lie. It's confusing, isn't it? The Underground is good, the Underworld is evil."

"I suppose," Devora said, longing to believe as strongly as Jaron. But she'd been tricked before …

"You have to trust, Devora. That's all we can do."

She nodded, and her thoughts wandered back to that nagging moment in the passageway several new moons ago. "But Gabria said—"

"Stop it, Devora! You can't tell me you would take the word of Gabria over Ansel?"

"I want to be sure. Maybe I could go back. Just to see."

"I'll go with you. Soon. When Ansel says it's okay, we'll go help the Underground together."

They carried the dishes inside Jaron's shelter and washed them. Soon Jaron nodded off to sleep beside the fireplace hearth and Devora covered him with a woven blanket before slipping outside.

"When *Ansel* says," she mimicked, her heart hammering in her chest. Jaron acted like they couldn't make a move without Ansel's approval. Well, she'd managed to look after herself all those years in the Heaps. What would the harm be in going back just to check?

She slipped inside her own shelter to gather a cloak and food. Dropping items into an embroidered bag, she hesitated. What was she forgetting? Her eyes locked on a knife she'd used earlier in the day. A weapon—she'd almost forgotten her need to defend herself!

Stepping into the night, she tugged her cloak close to stave off the chill. "I'll be back soon, Jaron," she whispered softly, hesitating. *I don't want to be alone again*, she thought. *But I have to know. I have to be sure.*

Perhaps she should have told the others what she'd heard. After all, she'd been the last to step through the door to home, the last to hesitate, lingering in the passageway—the only one of them to hear the faint echoing sound.

A baby's cry.

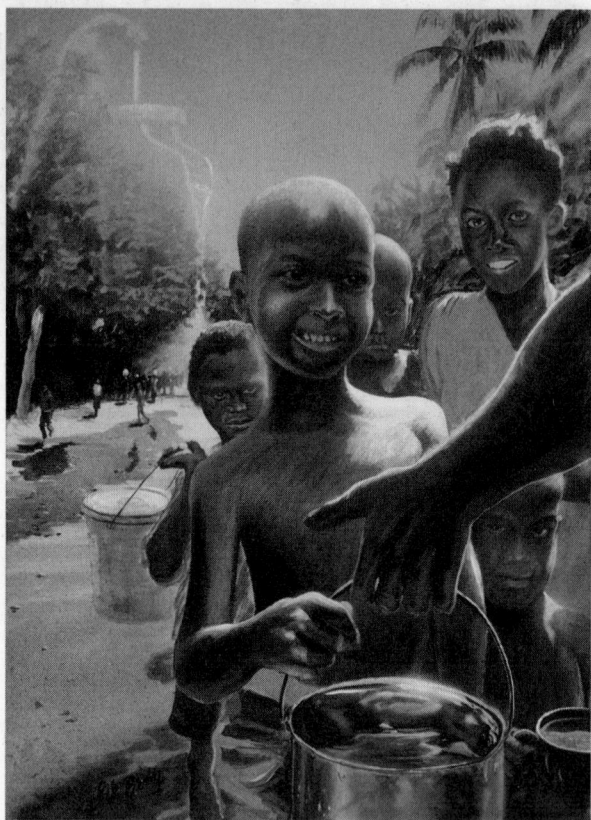

Cup of Cold Water Project

The Cup of Cold Water Project was birthed in 2001 when Evan Morgan walked 8,423.9 km across the entire nation of Canada. The purpose of this Guinness Record journey was to raise awareness and funds for providing water wells in Haiti.

About seventy-five percent of Haiti's population lives in abject poverty. The non-potable water in this impoverished country becomes a breeding ground for typhoid and cholera—diseases to which children are particularly susceptible. Access to safe water must be seen as a basic human right and a key factor in the fight against disease.

Over the years, the Cup of Cold Water Project has been continuing to provide water wells in many communities of Haiti. After the devastating earthquake of January, 2010, an added emphasis has been placed on earthquake relief to help rebuild Haiti.

Please check our website www.cupofcoldwater.org to see how you can become involved in blessing the nation of Haiti.

We can be contacted at:

Cup of Cold Water Project
147 Chandler Drive
Lower Sackville, NS B4C 1Y3
Phone: (902) 471-3333

Acknowledgements

I fell in love with reading at a very young age, yet the joy in the writing process did not take hold until much later—even now it often eludes me. However, although there is not always joy, there is an overwhelming passion within me to the calling of storytelling. When an idea grabs hold, it hangs on for dear life until I take notice and write it down. For this passion to create, I thank my Creator. I acknowledge that any good I might be, do, or ever become is from Him.

I never imagined that buying a palm-sized figurine in Old Warsaw in 1991 would, fifteen years later, inspire the beginnings of the Garbage Heaps of Leviathon. So, to that unknown artist in Poland who created the sculpture of the father and child huddled together with their loaf of bread, I say, "Thank you."

My own heritage, somewhat like Jaron's, has been richly blessed by those who have followed a path less travelled. My grandfathers, Rev. Dr. Ralph Lowe and Rev. Claude Morgan, were "Keepers of the Key" in their own right and though they have gone on to their reward, I am thankful for their legacy.

Evan and Donna Morgan, my parents, are two of the most unusual and inspiring people I have ever known. I have watched their lives illustrate how it is better to give than to receive. I am proud to be your daughter and I love you.

Matthew, you are a gift from God. That is what your name means and that is who you have become to me. My husband, my friend, a loving father to our children, I love you. Your support has made living my dreams possible.

The word "Mommy" never sounded like the song of angels until I heard it spoken by my two children. Joshua, you are my favourite boy! Elianna, you are my favourite girl! Both of you complete my life with love and laughter and you will always be my greatest accomplishment.

When I first walked into a writing workshop offered by the Writers Federation of Nova Scotia, I thought it was to take a daylong seminar. Almost a decade later, I have found writing support and friends to last a lifetime. I wish to give special thanks to Norene Smiley for helping me find my writing voice, and to Jo Ann Yhard for answering my daily phone calls. Many thanks also to the additional friends, family, and members of the Thursday Scribblers who have helped to shape my lumps of clay into stories.

Winning the contest offered by Word Alive Press has brought the dream of "Unlocked" into the reality of print. I am grateful to Jeremy, Caroline, and Larissa for your belief that this story had merit.

The day I received news of being a contest finalist was also the day my brother, Matthew, and I said our final goodbyes to our beloved *Poppie*. Thank you, Matthew, for your encouraging words during that roller coaster moment on Highway 103.

And finally, I wish to acknowledge my very best friend, Joan, who hates reading fiction but has promised to read my book to the very end. Just checking …

~Cynthia